CONSTABLE ABOUT
THE PARISH

Constable About the Parish

NICHOLAS RHEA

ROBERT HALE · LONDON

ISBN 0 7090 5896 9

Robert Hale Limited
Clerkenwell House
Clerkenwell Green
London EC1R 0HT

Photoset in North Wales by
Derek Doyle & Associates, Mold, Clwyd.
Printed in Great Britain by
St Edmundsbury Press Ltd, Bury St Edmunds, Suffolk.
Bound by WBC Book Manufacturers Limited,
Bridgend, Mid-Glamorgan.

1

'And hath determined the bounds of their habitation!'

Acts 17.26

One Saturday morning in early summer there was a light knock on the door of my police house at Aidensfield. I opened it to find the village schoolmistress standing there. Fairly new to the area, she was clutching a briefcase which suggested her arrival was for an official purpose. In her early thirties, petite, blonde and very pretty in her white blouse and red mini-skirt, Josie Preston smiled and said, 'Mr Rhea, I have been asked to organize the beating of the Aidensfield bounds and wondered if the police ought to be involved. I am hoping to get lots of people to perambulate around the parish boundaries, like they used to do in bygone times.'

'It sounds interesting, something for my diary of events,' I said. 'But a police presence usually depends on what's going to happen, whether public places or public roads are going to be used and how many people turn up. Come in and tell me about your ideas.'

I led her into my office, settled her on a chair and asked Mary to organize some coffee. Josie had joined the primary school as recently as last Easter and, after expressing a desire to contribute to village life, had very quickly been appointed clerk of the parish council;

already, she was tackling her out-of-school duties with flair and gusto.

Sipping her coffee, she told me that one of her intentions was to revive some of the old village customs, and a renewal of beating the Aidensfield bounds was one of her intentions.

'This is what it entails.' She produced a map from her briefcase and spread it across my desk, adding, 'Members of the parish council and the villagers will walk around the parish boundaries, halting from time to time to confirm certain markers, such as the Priest Oak and the Shaff Stone. They will make sure that every point on the boundary is visited and noted. The old custom was to beat the outermost point of our boundary by bumping it with the oldest and youngest persons who were taking part in the perambulation. It seemed like a bit of fun – they were lifted up by the legs and arms, then their bottoms were bumped on the ground. Our furthest point is the site of the Six Standing Stones on Howe Rigg Moor, so we'll rest there and have a picnic. In the other villages where the custom has continued, the bumping is done quite gently but it's a delightful way of making sure people do remember their parish boundaries.'

'After that kind of performance, I'm sure they'll never forget!' I laughed.

I knew something about the custom. It still took place in various parts of the country and in other districts of Yorkshire, even though it had been abandoned at Aidensfield long ago. There were several ways of beating the bounds; lots of parishes adopted a system similar to that used in Aidenfield, lifting young men by their arms and legs and bumping their bottoms at all the strategic places along the boundary.

In our case, we bumped at just one place – the most distant point. In some of the other rituals, away from Aidensfield, lads were held upside down so that their heads were bumped on the ground, but it was all done very gently with no hurt being caused, and the purpose was to ensure they never forget the extent of their own parish, should a dispute arise. Another quaint idea, still practised in some parishes, was for everyone to carry sticks and literally beat every boundary marker, be it a standing stone, a tree, a large boulder, building or other permanent fixture.

The hilarity thus created was another way of imprinting an indelible memory of the boundaries in the minds of the growing generation. Some parishes conduct these ceremonies once every seven years; others do so at more frequent intervals but in each case, the purpose is to impress the precise limits of the parish in the minds of the young.

Centuries ago, it was the custom to actually thrash the seats of the young men of the parish at the boundary markers, another way of ensuring they never forgot! In one Yorkshire parish, a boundary marker is a rock in the middle of a deep, fast flowing river and so the boundary has to be marked by the parish clerk hiring a boat and sailing out to tap the rock with a stick or else wading out in fishing boots. Streams which go underground, boundaries that pass through railway tunnels or through houses or those which are variable due to a high or low tide have given rise to some remarkable and memorable boundary-marking customs. One such custom on the North York Moors extends over two days – it is done on foot complete with picnic meals because the perambulation covers thirty hilly moorland miles. It is only done when the estate passes to a new member of the owning family who have owned it since Norman times.

In the case of Aidensfield, it seemed that Josie proposed to persuade the entire village to turn out, especially the children and teenagers, and for the event to be given the joyful flavour of a parish picnic or happy ramble with food and drink. She wanted everyone to tour the boundaries of the parish, halt at the necessary markers to note them, and then to witness the required ceremonial bumping at the Six Standing Stones.

A photographer would accompany the perambulators to record the event for posterity. Josie explained that the total distance would be around twelve miles, most of it over fields via public rights of way or across moorland by known tracks, although there would be some stretches where public roads would be used. That is when the police would become involved – if large numbers of people were to march or perambulate along public roads, then the road safety aspect had to be considered. The likelihood of danger from passing traffic had to be recognized. Another factor for consideration was access by emergency vehicles – there was always the possibility that some aged walker might collapse and require emergency hospital treatment.

But, bearing in mind all those factors, I felt sure there would be no objections from any of my senior officers and asked Josie to send me a written agenda when her plans had been finalized. She told me that a Sunday in August was the likely date. In the meantime, I would enter the details in all our official records and inform my superiors.

'Is it really necessary?' questioned Sergeant Blaketon, when I called at Ashfordly police station to tell him about the plans. 'It seems a lot of palaver for very little reason. Surely, the parish boundaries are not in doubt these days, they're clearly marked on local maps.'

'The civil parish boundaries are on the map, sergeant, not the ecclesiastical ones.'

'So which parish boundaries are they going to mark? Precisely which boundaries are we talking about?' he put to me, and I must admit I had not thought to clarify that with Josie.

'Well,' I said, 'now you've raised the point, I suppose there are three parishes at Aidensfield. The Anglican parish, the Catholic parish and the civil parish. Josie – Miss Preston – is clerk to the civil parish, sergeant, so I imagine she's planning to perambulate the civil boundaries.'

'Which is an unnecessary chore, like I said, because they are marked on the map,' was his response. 'We can see where the boundaries run. This is the 1960s remember. Such information is adequately recorded.'

'But it's a bit of fun, sergeant,' I said. 'A community effort. Surely the police would not wish to object to the idea?'

'Who said anything about objecting, Rhea?' I could see that his eyes were twinkling. 'All I am asking is precisely which parish boundary is to be marked so that I can establish, in my own mind, the reason for the event. Isn't this medieval performance done to prevent disputes? To instil in the minds of the young people the precise boundaries of their parish so that land-grabbers like Greengrass and his ilk do not usurp the freedom of individuals by fencing off open spaces, nicking common land or making false claims to the ownership of sheep grazing grounds?'

'Yes, something like that.'

'So if young John Willie gets bumped at the wrong place and marks the extent of a church parish boundary rather than the civil one, surely that would fuel greater arguments if a dispute did arise? He wouldn't know whether his bump was a civil one or a heavenly one. His bruised bum could conjure up memories of the wrong place, Rhea. Taking it further, if he went to court to argue the point and got it wrong, it could cause ecclesiastical havoc and civil unrest in Aidensfield. And I'm sure none of us wants that to happen.'

'I'll have words with Josie Preston, sergeant,' I assured him. 'But in principle, can I take it that we have no objections to the proposed perambulation?'

'We've no powers to prevent it, Rhea, but, of course, I have no objections provided there is due regard for the safety of everyone, especially when the walkers are on public roads,' he said. 'Indeed, I might even join the perambulation; it's one way of learning a bit about the landscape which is within my jurisdiction. But do make sure your perambulators know which boundaries they are supposed to be marking.'

I felt he had both scored a point and raised an important matter, so before returning to discuss the precise route with Josie, I did a little research of my own.

I learned that the three Aidensfield parishes each had a different boundary. One problem was that neither of the two ecclesiastical boundaries was very precisely determined. For the purposes of the Church of England, a

parish is defined as ordinarily a district committed to the
charge of one incumbent and, as the vicar of Aidensfield
cured souls in the neighbouring villages of Elsinby and
Maddleskirk, it seemed that the present Anglican parish
embraced all those villages plus an indeterminate slice of
land surrounding each of them. As a consequence, that
parish boundary was of considerable extent. Because there
were Catholic churches in Aidensfield, Elsinby and
Maddleskirk, each with their own priests, it seemed that
the Catholic parishes, although more numerous, were
individually smaller with each being restricted to a single
village, albeit with the inclusion of some outlying farms
and hamlets. On the other hand, the extent of the third
Aidensfield parish – the modern civil one – was based on
the parish that existed through a combination of Tudor
highway legislation and the Poor Relief Act of 1601.

Before 1927, a civil parish was an area for which a
separate poor rate was, or could be made, or where a
separate overseer was appointed. In very general extent, a
poor law parish covered the same ground and boasted
the same boundaries as the corresponding Church of
England ecclesiastical parish but by 1921 permanent
changes were occurring. The Church of England's
parishes were reducing in number while growing larger in
size and, at the same time, various Acts of Parliament were
determining areas which were linked for local government
purposes to the changes of county and district boundaries.
The effect of this was gradually to separate the civil
parishes from the Church of England's ecclesiastical
parish boundaries, and this was confirmed by the Rating
and Valuation Act of 1925. That Act specified that on 1
April 1927, the old system of rating based on the poor rate
levied by parishes would be abolished.

In this way, the ecclesiastical and civil parishes were
finally and officially separated although, in practice, in
rural areas this had occurred as early as 1894. By the time I
returned to Josie, I was sure that the parish boundaries she
wished to celebrate were those of the civil parish, even if
they were marked on the map. I realized that even if the
exercise had no legal effect, it would provide a wonderful

opportunity for a happy community gathering.

When I tried to clarify the matter with her, she smiled and said, 'PC Rhea, in this village I am aware of the various religious affinities of the people, and of their civic pride. So I did a little research of my own. Before the Reformation, the parish church was Catholic as you know, and it had its own parish boundaries. It was during that time that the beating of the Aidensfield bounds began. I haven't a precise date but it was sometime in the Middle Ages. After the Reformation, when our parish church was taken over by the state to accommodate the new faith, the Church of England in other words, the parish boundaries did not change. And now, if you check on a map of that time, you'll see that those early ecclesiastical boundaries are exactly the same as those of the present civil parish.'

'So we shall be perambulating three parish boundaries at one and the same time!' I realized. 'And all in exactly the same place?'

'Yes.' She smiled at me. 'That's why I think it is important for us to revive this old custom. I believe Aidensfield is unique in this – I have not found any other parish with such historic boundaries, boundaries that have survived when others have been subjected to lots of change and, in fact, the Anglican boundary *has* changed. The point I am making is that the present civil boundary marks the precise extent of the earlier ecclesiastical boundaries which were embraced by the old and new faiths.'

Having established that, I noted that the perambulation was planned for Saturday, 20 August commencing at 10.30 a.m. from the war memorial on the green. Josie and the parish council produced some attractive posters and advertisements in the local *Gazette* in the weeks prior to the event, and although it occurred in the midst of the school holidays, many families promised a day's outing to their children. I was scheduled to be on duty in Aidensfield that day, to accompany the procession around the boundaries with due regard for the safety of everyone. A rest period was scheduled from 1 p.m. until 2 p.m. at which time it was estimated the perambulators would reach the Six Standing Stones.

Those stones were the most prominent of the boundary markers and stood on the moors high above the village. The perambulators would remain for their picnic lunch and that is where the bumping ceremony would take place.

There was a steep, unmade track leading up to the Six Standing Stones and it was made clear that if anyone cared to join the perambulators at that point for the picnic and to witness the bumping ceremony, they would be welcome. The unsurfaced track to the Six Standing Stones was passable for motor vehicles, but only just! It was recognized that, because of the hilly and sometimes rough terrain, the elderly and infirm of Aidensfield would not be able to complete the walk but by having lifts to the Six Standing Stones they would be able to participate in the event and revive their own flagging memories.

The perambulation seemed to be well organized, so Mary, with my own little family, said she would drive up to the Six Standing Stones for the picnic and would take something for me to eat. It was too far to walk for the youngest of our four children.

The morning of the perambulation was bright, sunny and warm. It was a lovely August day, so typical of the best of an English summer with not a cloud in the sky, and yet the temperature high upon those moors could be quite chilly. In preparation, I went to the war memorial just after ten o'clock. I was in full uniform, albeit wearing a pair of stout walking boots, and was pleased to see that lots of families were gathering. Most of them seemed well equipped for the trek – they were village people who knew the quick-changing mood of the loftier moorland heights and they sported knapsacks full of food and drink. Mums and dads had brought along their children and very soon the gathering grew into a cheerful and noisy group of young people.

Josie was passing among them, counting heads and making sure that any children without their parents were suitably prepared for the long walk. And then, as the church clock ticked away the minutes, Claude Jeremiah Greengrass arrived in an ice-cream van. Alfred, his scruffy lurcher dog, was sitting in the passenger seat and the moment the van stopped, it was surrounded by eager youngsters. Claude lost no time opening his vehicle to dispense cooling cones and wafers to the gathering. I wandered across and bought a cone.

'I had no idea you were in the ice-cream business, Claude?' I wondered what sort of licence was required to run a mobile ice-cream business from a vehicle but that was no concern of mine. It was a council matter.

'It belongs to a pal of mine, Constable,' said Claude. 'He's gone to a funeral today, so he said I could use his van and sell the ice-cream. I'm off up to the Six Standing Stones later – after I've done Elsinby, Crampton and the rest of Aidensfield. It's a good day for ice-creams, Constable. I should do good business on those moors.'

'You're not attempting the walk then?'

'Me?' he burst. 'Not at my age, Constable! You'll not get any of the local folks with any sense tackling that walk on a hot day like this. It's climb, climb, climb all the way to them big stones on the moor top.... It's for youngsters, Constable, it's for fit folks under forty, I reckon. No good for pensioners. I'll be there to witness the bumping but I'll be in this van and I reckon I'll sell the whole vanful to those folks who reach them Six Standing Stones.'

Leaving him to his sales, I turned to see Sergeant Blaketon parking his police car outside the Aidensfield Stores. Looking as smart as ever, he strode across to me complete with walking stick and sturdy boots, then he beamed. 'I thought I would join you today, Rhea. It's a lovely day for a stroll in the countryside.'

'Delighted to have you with us, Sergeant,' I said, thinking it was more than a stroll.

'And is that Greengrass with that ice-cream van? Is the walk too much for him?' Then he bellowed across to his old adversary, 'Perambulation of the Aidensfield boundaries too much for you, is it, Greengrass?'

'When you've done that walk as many times as me,' retorted Claude, 'you'll know every stone along every inch of the way. What I don't know about Aidensfield parish boundaries could be written on your little fingernail, Sergeant Blaketon, with room to spare for the Lord's Prayer.'

'Well, I shall be going,' said Blaketon. 'I am not afraid to set an example to our younger friends!'

'Happen I might sell you an ice-cream when you reach the Six Standing Stones then?' beamed Claude.

'I might just indulge in one of your finest cones, Greengrass,' said Blaketon. 'That's if that creaking old truck of yours will survive the day!'

'And if those creaking old legs of yours survive half the day!' chuckled Claude, beaming to his amused audience.

I was then aware of Josie and other members of the parish council ushering everyone into a manageable group and one of them shouted, 'Right, everyone. Time to go. Keep together please, we don't want to lose anyone.'

And so the Perambulation and Beating of the Aidensfield Parish Boundaries got underway. Chattering happily we all formed a neat crocodile as Rudolph Burley, the auctioneer and current chairman of the parish council, led the way. I decided to take up a position at the rear of the procession in case there were any stragglers.

Sergeant Blaketon joined me, although from time to time he darted ahead to chat with some of the participants. I could see he was really enjoying himself; it was a total change from his usual office routine and he seemed more relaxed than normal. The children loved him.

It wasn't long before the heat of the day and the tough climb began to take its toll. The final mile or so to the summit, at well over 1300 feet, produced one of the steepest climbs within the North York Moors and some of the hikers had to halt and rest. Even the children were finding it tiring and I could see that Sergeant Blaketon, clad in his thick uniform as I was, was perspiring profusely but refusing to give in. He would show them that he was quite capable of leading the way to the Six Standing Stones and on several occasions, I saw him holding hands with some of the children to give them encouragement.

It was with some relief that we all arrived at the Six Standing Stones, albeit in varying stages of exhaustion.

The stones are a landmark for miles, each rising some

eight or ten feet from the ground and standing in a rough circle over an area about the size of a tennis court. The wind and weather had produced grotesque shapes upon some of them and the place was a popular picnic site with both locals and visitors. In the shadows of the stones, therefore, we sat on the dry grass and small rocks to gather our strength and to enjoy our picnic lunch. During our trek, Claude had arrived in his ice-cream van and was proving hugely popular as Alfred wandered around and sniffed the heather.

It wasn't long before the dog realized there were titbits on offer from some of the children, and this prompted him to stay around while the food was available. I took the opportunity to sit and enjoy a few moments with my own family, Mary having driven here with our brood of four and our picnics. Sergeant Blaketon was sitting with Rudolph Burley and they were enjoying a bottle of beer apiece; I saw one child carry to each of the venerable gentlemen a large ice-cream, a gift from Claude. It was a happy scene, nicely captured by the official photographer who had walked with us. I did a quick count and calculated that about sixty people were completing the walk, with a further thirty or so joining us at the Six Standing Stones. A turnout of almost a hundred villagers was very good in my estimation and so far there had been no incidents like nettled knees, twisted ankles or blistered feet.

Soon, the children began to gallop around among the Six Standing Stones, playing hide and seek and other chasing games, and that was the cue to resume the next stage of our journey. Josie shouted to them and gradually everyone packed their bags and prepared for the second half of the trek.

But before setting off, there was a formality to complete. It was time for the famous bumps.

'All right, everyone, it's time for the bumps. Six bumps in the middle of the Standing Stones. Now, we need the youngest person on the walk. Hugh Robinson, I think that will be you!' Josie's knowledge of the infant class was useful there.

'Yes, miss.' A small boy with freckles and carroty hair came forward, embarrassed but at the same time proud to be the one chosen for this important task.

'How old are you, Hugh?' Josie asked.

'Six and a quarter, miss.'

'Is there anyone younger than Hugh?' she asked of the gathering.

Among the perambulators, there wasn't anyone younger, although younger children had been brought to the picnic. Hugh was therefore escorted into the centre of the Stones and asked to lie down on the grass. Then, after explaining what they were going to do, two large men, members of the parish council, lifted him up by his hands and feet and gently bumped him six times on the ground. His mother and father stood by as the photographer took pictures and Hugh's pals cheered him – from that day, Hugh and his pals would never forget that the parish boundary extended to the centre of the Six Standing Stones. Hugh was applauded by all for his spirited participation.

'Now for the adults. It's the turn of the oldest man on the perambulation.'

I looked around the gathering.

Most of the men were in their late thirties and early forties, parents of the children, and I could not see anyone who might be described as elderly. As anticipated, the older folks had travelled by car to join the perambulators at the Six Standing Stones. The result was that no one came forward, but everyone looked at Rudolph Burley. As chairman of the parish council, he was the obvious choice.

'Nay,' he said. 'I did come here expecting to be bumped, but I see I'm not the oldest man on this perambulation. That's you, Sergeant Blaketon.'

'Me?' Sergeant Blaketon looked around as if he could not believe his ears. 'But I'm not a parishioner of Aidensfield, I don't qualify.'

'That is immaterial, Sergeant.' Josie had approached him and was smiling sweetly into his eyes. 'All that the custom demands is that the oldest man on the perambulation is bumped, not the oldest parishioner. The rule is quite clear.'

'Nobody told me that!' he spluttered.

I could see that poor old Blaketon was far from happy about this and he began to look around in despair, his eyes catching mine as he said, 'Do something, Rhea!'

'How old are you, Sergeant?' I asked.

''That's my private business,' he muttered.

'Go on, Blaketon, be a sport, get yourself bumped and make a bit of history....' Claude Jeremiah had left his ice-cream van to enjoy this situation. 'Now you know why I didn't do the walk....'

'This has nothing to do with you, Greengrass!' bellowed Blaketon.

'Right.' I had to try and calm the situation and tried to act as mediator. 'I reckon it's between you, Sergeant, and Rudolph, so if you both write your birthdays on a piece of paper and give them to Josie, she will decide who is the oldest and she will keep your precious secrets. No cheating, mind!'

They agreed with my plan and as I had some paper in my pocket, I gave a piece to each man.

Rudolph scribbled on his and passed it to Josie, closely followed by Blaketon. She studied the dates and said, 'It is you, Sergeant Blaketon. You are three months older than Mr Burley.'

'Bump Sergeant Blaketon, bump Sergeant Blaketon!' Claude began to chant.

The children took up the challenge, swiftly followed by Alfred barking in unison. Soon the ring of stones and the moorland air was filled with the music of children, young and old, chanting as Sergeant Blaketon, blushing furiously and trying to appear nonchalant, walked forward for his ordeal. He took off his uniform cap and jacket, handing them to me for safe keeping, and I knew that he had no wish for himself to be photographed in uniform while undergoing this treatment.

'Come on, do your worst!' he called, and four sturdy men came forward. He lay on the ground and extended his arms and legs for the bumpers to seize, and then to the cheers of everyone and to the barking of Alfred the dog, he was ceremoniously raised and lowered until his buttocks touched the ground. The requisite six bumps were achieved with much sweating and groaning from the volunteers but as Sergant Blaketon got to his feet, everyone cheered.

Then the children held hands and danced around him. Alfred chased them, barked, entering the spirit of the occasion.

'We like the sergeant, we like the sergeant,' they began to sing, as Alfred began to howl at the noise produced by their piping voices. Suddenly, it was all over and I handed him his cap and jacket.

'You did well, Sergeant.' I had to say something.

'If you tell Ventress or any of the others about this....'

'Sergeant.' It was Rudolph Burley. 'That was very good of you, to enter the spirit of the occasion like that. I congratulate you.'

The adulation he had received now made Sergeant Blaketon feel much happier and he muttered something about the police supporting community projects. As the perambulators gathered to begin the second section of their trek, those who had joined us at the Stones gathered to wave us off. They would go home soon, I was sure; already Mary was packing our car with the remnants of our picnic and Claude was preparing to move his ice-cream van to another location. Once the people returned to their homes, word of the Sergeant's part in this renewal of beating the bounds would get around and his part would be appreciated. And as I watched him walking ahead surrounded by happy children and parents, I was proud of him.

'He's like the Pied Piper of Hamlyn,' I said to Rudolph, as we began the second section of the journey. 'See how those kids are following him.'

'Underneath that stern official skin, there's a real human being, isn't there?' he smiled.

'That's what being a police officer is all about,' I said, striding forward.

2

'Cursed shall be the flocks of thy sheep'

Deut. 28.18

For more years than anyone could remember, Emily Jane Taylor, a spinster of the parish of Aidensfield, had tended the graves in the Anglican churchyard. She spent hours there, always alone. On hot days, cold days, wet days and dry days she could be seen throwing out dead flowers, adding water to empty vases and even cleaning the tombstones when she felt it necessary. She clipped the yews and trimmed the hedges, and for years had mown the grass, initially with a scythe and later with a motor mower which had been donated by a benefactor. It was due to her efforts, and hers alone, that the churchyard was always in such pristine condition, an oasis of admirable tidiness.

It was one of the few churchyards in the vicinity which could be guaranteed neat and tidy upon every day of the year. It was a place of pride for the villagers and a source of joy for visitors. There is little doubt that the immaculate condition of Aidensfield churchyard helped to swell the coffers of the church, because suitably impressed visitors would mark their appreciation by dropping coins into the offertory box. That income, over the course of a year, was considerable and the church depended upon it.

For all sorts of reasons, therefore, Emily Jane was a

treasure. Members of the congregation who had suffered the loss of dear ones knew that the graves would be cared for year after year with little or no effort on their part. Their mourned ones would not be neglected when the living were on holiday or after their initial distress had dwindled into forgetfulness or even downright neglect. Somehow, Emily Jane managed to find flowers for all the graves, even though bereaved families forgot to supply them in the passage of time.

No one was quite sure of Emily Jane's age – certainly, she was well past fifty and might even have been in her seventies but she had always appeared very fit, healthy and active. She enjoyed a modest but independent income and led a contented lifestyle, even though she had never married. Her mode of dress – a battered old raincoat, wellington boots and a multicoloured woolly hat with a pompom – prompted some to believe she was eccentric or, as some might put it, ten pence to the shilling. Yet her mind was alert and in spite of her Arcadian appearance, she was devoted to the churchyard and its peaceful occupants. Indeed, it was her main activity.

So thorough and dependable was she that both the parochial church council and the congregation were content to leave the care of the grounds to Emily Jane. She was allowed to perform her self-imposed tasks without anyone instructing or guiding her, even though her constant devotion was something of a mystery to the rest of us. For one thing, she never attended church and showed no interest in religious matters and, so far as anyone knew, she had no family or relatives in Aidensfield churchyard. Indeed, to our knowledge, she had no family anywhere, living or dead. There was one rumour, however, which suggested she had once been in love.

Some people hinted that her youthful heart's desire had either died in his twenties or been killed in the First World War. Others said that her lover was a local man who was buried here – having discarded Emily Jane to marry someone else – and that Emily Jane had committed herself to his grave for the rest of her days. To keep his name a secret from the world, she tended all the graves so that no one should ever know to which she was truly devoted ... but even that yarn had never been substantiated. Certainly, I had no idea about the dramas or romances in her life prior to my arrival at Aidensfield.

My own contact with her came during my regular checks on the church treasures. From time to time, wandering villains plundered quiet village churches, emptying the offertory boxes or even stealing brass candlesticks from the altar, sometimes extending their thieving to other valuables like antique chairs or tables.

In spite of the risks, which seemed to increase by the year, everyone was loath to lock the church doors and consequently security was something of a worry. I made it my policy to be seen, in uniform, in or near all the churches on my patch at very frequent but irregular intervals; it was a modest form of deterrent, but better than nothing. It was during such visits that I encountered Emily Jane. At first, she ignored my presence, preferring to work quietly without any interruption from me, but when I realized who she was and what she was doing, I made a point of introducing myself. To help me in my job and to protect the parish treasures for the benefit of all, she could be the eyes and ears of Aidensfeld church, a real-life guardian angel.

Once I had made the initial approach, she would pause during her labours for a chat with me, telling me about the people in her care, the history of the church, who had been popping into the building either for a look around or simply to offer a quiet prayer. Over the months, I became quite fond of the untidy little woman and realized she had a very sharp and well-tutored mind. She was well read, well bred and well educated and, in spite of the speculation about her motives, we all regarded her work for the churchyard as a most valuable contribution to the community.

If she had a weakness, though, it was her language. Practically every sentence contained several swear words, some of a moderately mild nature and others which were more fitted to a life on the ocean wave or a rugger club's changing-room. I had never heard anyone swear quite like her, but I don't think she realized what she was saying. I don't think she ever considered it might be offensive to some of the more refined listeners of the parish or to casual visitors. Another associated problem was that she talked to herself as she worked, consequently visitors to the churchyard might hear a strong female voice, somewhere out of sight behind a tombstone, saying, 'I'll make ****** sure this ****ing grave has ****ing flowers on it before I go home' or 'Where's the ****ing watering can gone now?'

Such entertainment did not interest or unduly trouble most of the locals. Even the most sensitive people tolerated Emily Jane's choice language because all knew her very well indeed.

She used the same language in the shop or when visiting friends and they understood that it was never intended to be inflammatory or rude. And, after a time, I must admit I grew accustomed to hearing her flowery language and rarely gave it a second thought, although I hoped she would modify it when children were nearby. Under the Profane Oaths Act of 1745, still in force, it was an offence to profanely curse or swear, while the Town Police Clauses Act of 1847 also made it illegal to use profane or obscene language in any street or urban place to which the public had access. In addition, there were byelaws which sought to control bad language but to prosecute her would have seemed rather heavy handed, particularly as no one ever lodged a formal complaint about Emily Jane's vocabulary.

Then, one summer afternoon, I called at the Anglican parish church and heard her voice, this time louder and more vociferous than at any previous time. The range of impious oaths which were emanating from behind a yew tree were enough to turn the air blue for miles around. When I went to investigate the cause, I found Emily Jane. She was directing her anger and disrespectful language towards the silent lawnmower.

It was stubbornly refusing to start and she was venting her frustration in a very sailor-like manner. I offered to examine it for her – it was a very ancient piece of machinery and I suspected there were problems with the flow of fuel. The two-stoke mixture was not getting through – dirt in the fuel pipe or in the carburettor was the probable reason, but in any case the lawnmower was well beyond repair. Like poor old Emily Jane, it had almost reached the end of its useful time on this earth.

As we pondered the cause of the problem, she levelled a well-aimed kick at the mutinous machine and said, 'I'm going to ****ing well retire,' she announced with determination. 'They can get some other daft ****** to cut the ****ing grass.'

It was at this very moment that another character arrived on the scene. He was Laurie Cunningham, a keen churchgoer, church warden and member of the parochial church council. Like Emily Jane, he was retired, having been a stationmaster at Elsinby, and he spent a lot of his spare time in and around the church, a sort of self-appointed caretaker. A tall, bald man with a domed head and rounded spectacles, he enjoyed doing running repairs to the building. He liked to work with his hands, making things that might be useful such as a rack for hymn books or a metal boot-scraper to remove mud from the feet of the incoming congregation. He oiled the hinges of the door when it squeaked, repaired minor damage, cleared gutters, fixed leaks, replaced tiles and mended fences. Laurie was another asset to the church because he performed a whole range of useful, money-saving chores, often at his own expense. Like Emily Jane, he was often to be seen working around the church during the daylight hours.

' 'Morning, Mr Rhea. Emily Jane having bother again, is she?' and he smiled knowingly.

'I think the lawnmower's decided to retire,' I said.

'The ****** thing's not retired, it's dead on its feet,' she grinned. 'It's me who's going to ****ing well retire. Some other daft ****** can cut the grass from now on.'

'Emily, you can't. If you go, who else will take on this work? You've always made such a good job of the churchyard....' Laurie was devastated at her news.

But he knew, and I knew, that once Emily Jane had made up her mind, she would not retract her decision. It was very clear that, from this moment in Aidensfield's long history, someone else would have to cut the grass which encircled All Saints Church.

'I'll still tend the ****** graves,' she said, knowing what was going through Laurie's mind. 'I can still find some ****** flowers and keep the ******* water topped up. But as for the grass, well, that's for the ****ing PCC to sort out.'

And she stomped away, leaving the lawnmower where it was.

'Leave it with me, Mr Rhea,' Laurie said quietly. 'I'm sure we can find a volunteer and I'm equally sure we can obtain another lawnmower, a good second-hand one will do.'

But in Aidensfield as well as other villages of comparable size, finding volunteers is never easy. In spite of requests from the pulpit and notices in the window of the Aidensfield Stores, no one came forward. As Emily Jane continued to renew the flowers on the graves and replenish their water supplies, the grass around them grew longer. Weeds began to flourish and it wasn't long before the churchyard began to appear neglected. A local businessman did donate a replacement lawnmower, a very fine second-hand model, but no one appeared to have the time or willingness to use it on a permanent basis.

Although people did cut the grass from time to time, there was no permanent arrangement and very soon, Aidensfield churchyard assumed the appearance of an abandoned meadow rather than a well-kept lawn. To maintain it in its former glory required more than the occasional half-hour once a month. It had to be trimmed regularly; it needed another Emily Jane, but the village didn't have one.

It could be argued that such matters are no concern of the constabulary but, as a resident of the village, it was my wish that something was done, even if I did not have the time to regularly cut the grass. Besides, this wasn't my church – I belonged to the Catholic church, but I did trim the Anglican grass from time to time. Its sad state did cause some concern, particularly when there was a funeral or wedding but in spite of those requirements, no full-time volunteer was forthcoming. Laurie, other members of the PCC and several villagers did their turns, of course, but it was a hit-and-miss system and far from satisfactory.

It was a Thursday afternoon, while emerging from the churchyard via the lychgate, that I chanced to meet Claude Jeremiah Greengrass. I had completed a routine security check and he was pottering along the main street with Alfred his dog on a lead. Seeing me, he stopped for a chat. Even he was concerned about the state of the churchyard.

'Have they got summat done about that churchyard?' He nodded towards the lush deep grass behind the wall.

'Not yet, Claude,' I said. 'No one seems to have the time.'

'It's not time that's needed, it's sheep. Moor sheep. They'd trim it in less time than it takes you to buy me a pint,' he said. 'See how they keep the grass trimmed beside the moor roads?'

'You mean you'd turn them loose in the churchyard?'

'Why not? There's no finer thing for trimming grass. And they'd cost nowt.'

I recalled a previous occasion when sheep had been drafted into this very churchyard for grass-cutting duties. The vicar at the time, Roger Clifton, hadn't thought to make sure that the walls were sheep-proof, and the four-legged mowing machines had escaped to invade Rudolph Burley's prize flower garden. For a time, those sheep, and the idea of using them to keep the churchyard tidy, were rather unpopular.

Nonetheless, the grass shearing abilities of unfenced-in sheep of the North York Moors are widely known and admired. Villages like Hutton-le-Hole, Goathland, Castleton, Danby and Glaisdale are noted for their smooth grass verges and neatly trimmed greens, all done by the free-ranging blackfaced moorland sheep. The grass is as smooth as a bowling green, the only problem being that sheep cannot distinguish between private gardens and open moorland. In addition to Rudolph's flowers, other villagers have, over the years, suffered the loss of their prize collections of flowers and vegetables in this way. The villagers of the moorland communities have therefore learned the wisdom of having stout fences and well-maintained gates.

'They'd eat all the flowers on the graves!' I put to Claude.

'Not if the sheep were fenced in,' he returned. 'Fence a part of the graveyard off and put half a dozen ewes inside the fence. When they've mown that bit, shift the fence to another spot and let 'em do that bit, and so on until you've covered the whole lot. You don't need a permanent fence, just a length of high wire which can be spiked into the ground and held upright as it's made into a pen. Summat easily moveable is what you want. Farmers do it all the time with their livestock.'

'Doing the churchyard piece by piece, patch by patch, would take a long time,' I suggested.

'All right. Get Emily Jane not to put flowers on the graves for a week or so, to let the sheep have the run of the place. Bring the sheep in, say, once a month for grass cutting. Let 'em do the lot all at one go.'

'Maybe we could make some protective flower guards?' I suggested. 'Something like a large wire cloche, big enough to fit over a big vase full of tall flowers or a grave?'

I envisaged something about the size and shape of a bottomless dustbin made from wire and having spikes, say four of them, around the bottom edge. It could be placed over a vase of flowers on a grave, the spikes being pressed into the ground to secure it and thus save the precious flowers from the ruminations of the sheep. I told Claude I would mention it to Laurie Cunningham and within a few days, I encountered him in the village street. I mentioned Claude's idea of using sheep to mow the churchyard.

'Its been done before,' he said. 'Not without problems. They do a very good job but the snag is they chew everything. You've got to keep all the graves free of flowers while they're busy, and keep the church door shut otherwise they'll wander inside and make a mess. Getting visitors to shut gates and doors is impossible, Nick, they ignore signs and never use common sense. They're a bit like sheep in that respect – follow my leader and all that! And I must remind you that some folks aren't over-chuffed at the idea of a sheep mowing the grass which covers their great Aunt Jemima. And old Mrs Meldrew never did like mutton, she made that very clear when they sided her away.'

I mentioned the suggestion of a sheep-proof flower guard for each grave and made a rough sketch for Laurie to help explain my idea. Laurie, regarding himself as something of a handyman, said he would consider it and then refer the matter to the parochial church council. Shortly afterwards, I met the recently appointed vicar, the Reverend Christian Lord, at a coffee morning for the Red Cross and he said, 'Ah, Nick, Laurie has produced an idea to cope with the wilderness around the church,' he smiled. 'He tells me it originated through you. So I am thanking you, on behalf of us all.'

'Actually, it was Claude Jeremiah who first suggested the sheep,' I said.

'A good idea, but I mean the flower guards,' he said. 'The PCC has decided that if we can produce between a dozen and twenty of them, we can protect the grave-top flowers on a rota system, with the agreement of Emily Jane, and then we can introduce a small flock of ewes to carry out the task of mowing the grass for us.'

'Make sure the sheep don't escape over the walls into people's gardens,' and I reminded him of the last time this had been tried.

With the vicar's enthusiastic approval, Laurie soon produced his prototype flower guard. He had made it himself using four lengths of stout metal wire which were welded to an X shaped support at the top. The X was about two feet six inches from tip to tip, with a length of wire welded to each tip at right angles. Each length of wire was about four feet long, thus he had a squarish frame which was four feet tall and some two feet six inches wide at all points. Around this frame he fastened some chicken wire. He left four lengths of stout wire protruding about six inches from the surrounding rim at the bottom of the cage to form legs; these legs could be pressed into the earth and so the contraption would fit over the gravetop flowers and protect them from the sheep. The guard was large enough to accommodate something like a rosebush on top of a grave and was almost big enough to accommodate some of the smaller tombstones as well as the flowers.

I was told that the first fitting of the flower guard would occur on Wednesday next at half past ten in the morning, so I went along. With the vicar, Emily Jane, Laurie Cunningham and a few others, I stood and watched as Laurie fitted his flimsy contraption over a large ceramic pot containing a bunch of irises which was perched upon a grave. Gently, Laurie pressed the slender feet into the soft earth and the guard stood firmly in position, enough to defy the most determined sheep or rabbit. And it protected its wares.

Emily Jane spoke. 'So you *******s want me to work around those ****** things?'

Laurie was patient with her. 'What we are suggesting, Emily Jane, is that we place, say, a dozen or perhaps twenty of these guards around the graves bearing the freshest flowers. Then we can let the sheep in and they can work undisturbed for a few days to produce that lovely shorn look on the grass. At the right moment, you can put fresh flowers on some other graves, and we can repeat the process, allowing the sheep to graze those graves you tended earlier ... the guards are very light and portable, they can be easily moved around to suit our requirements and we need to have the sheep in at intervals, say once a fortnight or so. I do not envisage them being with us permanently.'

'It's a very positive solution to our problem, Emily Jane,' said the Reverend Lord.

The fact that the entire decision about the future mowing of the grass now depended upon the reaction of Emily Jane Taylor gave me some indication of her importance to the church authorities, and so we all awaited her reaction.

'It's going to be a bloody chore, shifting those ****** wire cages around, but if it means the damned place looks tidy, then I'll ******* well do it.'

The feeling of relief among us all was tangible and it seemed that a suitable compromise had been reached. Laurie went off to produce more of his guards, Emily Jane went back to her flower-tending, the vicar went off to visit a sick parishioner and I resumed my patrol.

I experienced a great feeling that the village was returning to normal. Within a week, the first volunteers of churchyard-mowing sheep were in action. They were a dozen blackfaced moorland ewes which belonged to Gordon Saddler of Moor End Farm and he was happy that they should perform this holy task. In fact, one of them had been blessed by the vicar at the last Harvest Thanksgiving, thus that particular animal was adequately qualified for its divine mission. Meanwhile, Laurie had manufactured a few more of his patent plant protectors and Emily Jane had, albeit with a little reluctance, consented to the format of this planned grass-mowing operation.

About a fortnight later, I was patrolling Aidensfield on foot and decided to pay my customary security visit. Pushing through the swing gate, I noticed that the grass inside was beautifully shorn, as good or even better than after the efforts of Emily Jane. In the far right-hand corner of the churchyard I could see eight or nine wire cages which had been erected over a selection of the newest graves, and in the area before the tower were a handful of contented ewes, ten or so, I estimated, all munching merrily at the lush feast before them. It seemed that the operation was highly successful and I knew that Gordon Saddler changed his sheep every few days on a rota system. I entered the church, checked that the offertory box had not been attacked and that the other artefacts were present and correct, and then resumed my patrol. But as I made my exit from the porch, I heard, from somewhere at the back of the churchyard, the distinctive tones of Emily Jane shouting, 'Get away you daft old ****, sod off!'

I wondered, for the briefest of moments, whether Laurie was getting too frisky with her, but decided it wasn't him, even if she did admire his wire plant protectors. I paused and listened, and then she cried again.

'Sod off ... you stupid bloody animal ... you ****ing lunatic ... clear off ... help! Is anybody there ... help!'

It was the cry for help that sent me running towards Emily Jane and I found her crouched behind a tombstone with a sheep standing and staring at her. It was a ewe, but blackfaced ewes are fitted with a useful pair of horns and this one had adopted a very antagonistic stance, glaring at Emily Jane as a bull might stare at a matador.

'Don't move!' I shouted as if I knew what to do next.

'Don't you worry yourself, Mr Rhea, I'm not ****** moving while it's looking at me like that ... ger off ... you ******* animal....'

The sheep made a move as if to attack her, but stopped after a step or two, apparently puzzled by the tombstone which served as a shield for Emily Jane. As she cringed on the ground peering over the top of the tombstone, her eyes stared into the face of the sheep as if she was trying to outstare a lion. Endeavouring to be brave, I went towards the sheep and shooed it off, waving my arms and shouting and, much to my surprise and relief, it backed off, turned away and trotted off quite amicably to rejoin its companions.

'You can get up now, Emily Jane,' I said, reaching out a hand to help her to her feet.

'They shouldn't allow such ****** dangerous animals to be let loose!' she grunted. 'Here am I, doing my ****ing best for this **** of a village and that ****** ewe goes for me.'

Even as she spoke, the ewe turned around and galloped towards her, its yellow eyes looking fierce against the smooth black of its face. Emily yelled in fright and once again sought the security of the tombstone as the sheep came towards her, then stood and gazed solemnly at her while she crouched in fear. For what seemed an eternity, ewe and woman stared at each other, neither moving as each tried to gauge the next move by the other. I went to

Emily's rescue again, shooing away the silly animal which, when I approached it, trotted off without any sign of antagonism. I made sure it was well away from Emily before I signalled for her to rise to her feet and join me.

'Are you frightened of it?' I put to her, knowing that some animals can smell fear in humans, a scent which makes them react fiercely against the person who is afraid.

'I can't honestly say I love the bloody thing,' she whispered the words. 'But I'm not frightened of *******
ewes if that's what you mean. I mean, Constable, I've lived among the ******* things all my life and I've been working my ****ing fingers to the bone in this ****** churchyard among all those **** looking animals and not one has bothered me, until that ****** came. No, it's that one. It hates me.'

'Come on, I'll take you out; you've finished here, have you, for today?'

'Aye, I'll go home now,' she consented in a very tiny voice. 'I've just got to put this ******* watering can in its usual ******* place.'

She did so, then as I walked with her towards the lychgate, she turned to look with some apprehension towards the group of grazing sheep, none of which paid the slightest attention to us. At this point, it was impossible to identify the rogue one – it had rejoined its companions to become anonymous.

When we reached the gate, Emily Jane turned and shouted at the sheep, 'Well, that's a ****, I've never been driven out by a ******* sheep before....'

And at that moment, the ewe detached itself from the flock and galloped towards Emily Jane; in a trice, she had slipped through the turnstile gate and was safe beside me as the ewe stood at the other side to peer up at her.

'It doesn't like you swearing,' I joked.

'Don't be bloody daft, Constable,' she said. 'It's just ******* well doesn't like me! I'm not going back in that ******* churchyard while it's at ******* well at large, I can tell you.'

As she spoke the sheep glared at her, but this incident meant we now had a beautifully mown churchyard but no one to tend the graves, unless that particular ewe was isolated and banished from the grounds. I mentioned it to Laurie Cunningham who said he'd have words with Gordon to try and ensure that no dangerous sheep were brought here for churchyard-mowing duties.

It would be a day or two later that I met Laurie in the street and asked, 'Did you get the matter of the rampant ewe sorted out?' I asked him.

'You're not going to believe this,' he grinned. 'But I had a word with Gordon and he fell about laughing.'

'Try me,' I was intrigued now.

'That ewe used to be a pet lamb. It was the usual story. The mother died and the lamb was reared on the farm by the family. But they had a labourer who ill-treated it. It was a long time before the kids found out what he was doing, but he would kick and attack the lamb while they weren't around – and he'd curse and swear as he did so. So that sheep has grown up to be afraid of people who swear – if anyone swears when it's around, it goes for them!'

I laughed and asked, 'So have you told Emily Jane?'

'I have, and she cursed me loud and long, but she has promised not to swear in the churchyard any more, just in case that sheep hears her.'

'I never thought anyone could stop her swearing, let alone a silly old ewe!' I laughed. 'Unless, of course, it was the Lamb of God!'

'There's many a true word ...' he laughed.

3

'I know thee to be expert in all customs and questions.'

Acts 26.3

'Rhea,' Sergeant Blaketon said as I answered the telephone one morning as I was about to leave the police house for a morning patrol. 'Meet me outside All Saints in Aidensfield, will you? Half past ten.'

'Very good, Sergeant,' I responded, wondering about the purpose of this rendezvous. Usually, he arranged to meet me at a village telephone kiosk or some other innocuous place, but a meeting outside the church heralded a departure from the norm. I was curious to learn his purpose and so, a few minutes before the appointed place and time, I parked my minivan outside the church.

' 'Morning, Rhea.' He was precisely on time as I'd come to expect, and seemed very bright and cheerful. 'A very pleasant day. All quiet in Aidensfield, its it?'

'Yes it is, Sergeant, very quiet,' I responded.

'Greengrass behaving himself, is he?' was his next, not entirely unexpected question.

'I've no problems recently,' I assured him, now wondering if Claude Jeremiah Greengrass was the reason for our meeting.

'And I see that your churchyard is in splendid condition, neatly cut and well maintained.'

'We have a very reliable grass-cutting system, Sergeant, we're all very proud of our churchyard. It's a credit to the village.'

'And rightly so,' he smiled. 'Well, you'll be wondering why I am here, so I had better tell you. There is to be a wedding at this church, next month, Saturday the eighteenth, if my information is correct?'

'Yes, that's true.' I had a note of the wedding in my diary. There would be a need for a police presence, if only to prevent traffic jams and obstruction in the narrow road outside the church. 'It's a young lady from Aidensfield, Sergeant, a Miss Valerie Perry-Smith. She is to marry a gentleman called Fenton, Howard Fenton I believe. He's a major in The Green Howards.'

'You're up to-date with your information, Rhea, and that pleases me. Now, you know who she is, do you? This Valerie Perry-Smith?'

'Yes, she's the daughter of Mr and Mrs Bruce Perry-Smith of the Gables, Aidensfield. He is a company director in the brewing industry; Mrs Perry-Smith does not work, although she does a lot for local charities.'

'All very enlightening, Rhea, but I meant the girl's connections. Do you realize to whom she is related?'

I began to wonder where this quiz was leading but it was evident that Miss Perry-Smith had some very important relations and it was equally evident that they would be coming to her wedding. I began to wonder if there were royal connections, or whether the young lady had links with the government or someone in high office such as the sheriff of the county or the Lord Chief Justice.

'No, Sergeant,' I had to admit. 'I don't know the family background all that well.'

'She is the niece of the chief constable no less,' he told me in hushed tones, as if he was imparting a major secret. 'That means he and his wife will be attending that wedding, Rhea, and you know what that means?'

I was tempted to say it would mean the presence of Sergeant Blaketon in his best uniform, with his hair neatly trimmed and his boots brightly polished. He would want to show everybody, but especially the chief constable, that the police of Ashfordly and Aidensfield were the smartest for miles around and quite capable of controlling traffic at such a prestigious event. But I took a deep breath and said, 'It means I shall have to be present outside the church to make sure everything goes smoothly, especially from a traffic and crowd-control point of view. I do have the date in my diary, Sergeant, and shall make sure my duties allow me to be present.'

'Good, I knew I could rely on you, Rhea. Now, for that day, I would suggest you get yourself a decent haircut, wear your best uniform brushed and pressed to perfection with not a cat hair in sight, and you should make sure your boots are polished until you can see your face in them. Furthermore, you should have well-prepared plans for car-parking and for whatever occurs outside the church and in the village street. Contingency plans, Rhea, a course of action already prepared ... be professional, Rhea, a lot depends on you. With the chief constable present, we need to present ourselves as perfection itself. Not a thing must go wrong, Rhea, is that understood?'

'Perfectly, Sergeant.' I felt like saying that most of the problems were the responsibility of the best man and wanted to add that the chief constable, in his off-duty moments, would not be interested in my role at the wedding. He'd be far too engrossed in family matters to bother about what I was doing. So long as things went smoothly without any major problem with traffic, he would be happy, I was sure. My own view was that a low-key police presence was advisable.

'His wife and Mrs Perry-Smith are sisters, Rhea, that's the relationship. Very nice people, the Perry-Smiths ... they're going to have the reception in a marquee in the grounds of their house. I know about it because George at the pub has applied for an occasional licence to run a bar at the event, after the first round of free drinks and champagne, of course.'

'I'm sure George will not cause me any problems,' I said. 'He can cope with any trouble-makers without my intervention. Besides, I don't expect a drunken orgy, not with this family and their guests. And I don't think we need worry about official police visits to the drinks tent while the chief constable is there.'

But Blaketon wasn't listening. 'You know, Rhea, this might be the biggest social event in the district this year. A society wedding, eh? An ideal opportunity to show the quality of the local constabulary to people of standing and influence. Thinking about it, Rhea, I might just arrange my duties so that I am available on the day, here with you, to help you, to supervise the arrangements and to ensure good order and tranquillity at all times.'

'I am sure there will be no problems, Sergeant.' I groaned under my breath at the prospect of his interference. 'I've had similar weddings at this church, several bigger than this one will be, and none has caused any problems. There's a need for a bit of traffic control on the main road as the guests are arriving and leaving the church, but that's all. I can manage very easily on my own, thanks.'

Knowing Blaketon's attitude towards people he considered to be influential, I realized there was no way I could prevent him performing his duty at the wedding. He wanted to be there, he wanted to present himself to the chief constable as a man who could organize a very efficient operation, even if that operation consisted of nothing more than a few minutes of very low-key traffic control. To be honest, there was no real need for a police presence at all, but in a village it is always good to show the uniform on such occasions. Even so, I knew the villagers would never object to a few minutes' traffic congestion outside the church if a wedding was the reason. But Blaketon wanted to impress someone and so, after our brief meeting, we examined the church, the street outside and the adjoining open spaces which could be utilized as car-parking areas. Having imparted his advice, Sergeant Blaketon left me.

In the ensuing weeks, he continued to remind me about the wedding and mentioned that, on a recent occasion, he had been to Force Headquarters where he had actually encountered the chief constable in one of the corridors. He had taken the opportunity to tell the chief that preparations for the efficient conduct of his niece's wedding were in hand. I groaned. Blaketon had no style. I would have thought the chief would not have wanted any police officer to attend that wedding – I felt he would prefer a relaxed occasion without any of his subordinates being in a position to observe his off-duty behaviour.

As the date approached, the father of the bride came to see me about car-parking and to discuss the other arrangements in which I might be involved, such as the security of the wedding presents. I outlined my plans and explained how I proposed to deal with the guests' cars on the day, saying that spaces had been reserved close to the church for the official cars. I assured him I would remain in and around the marquee so long as the presents were vulnerable and gave him some suggestions for their added security. He said my overall scheme was very sensible and practical, and then he invited me to join the guests in the marquee for something to eat and drink during the reception. He gave me an invitation card and promised that a place would be set aside for me.

It meant that I was to be a guest at the wedding, a real guest!

I thanked him; I would look forward to that, and knew that Mr Perry-Smith's action would have been approved by the chief constable. In effect, it gave me a rare opportunity to have a drink of alcohol while on duty ... but there was no mention of a similar invitation to Sergeant Blaketon. I thanked him again and we parted, but I decided not to mention either my invitation or my present-guarding duties to the sergeant. The days raced forward and the day of the wedding arrived very quickly. The time of the wedding service was 3 p.m., with guests beginning to assemble at the church shortly after 2 p.m.

After lunch, therefore, I changed into my smart best uniform, gave my shoes an extra polish and made sure no stray strands of hair were poking from my cap. I reckoned I was smart enough both to park cars and guard wedding presents, and off I went, walking instead of taking my official van. That would be one less vehicle to take up valuable parking space and, should I be offered chamapagne or wine, there would be no worries about drinking alcohol and then driving.

When I arrived at the church, the best man and ushers were already there. I outlined my part in the event, explaining how they could help me guide the cars to their allocated parking places with emphasis upon keeping all traffic moving. They understood perfectly. Happy that there would be no major hitches, I settled down to guide the procession of cars into their parking places. And then Sergeant Blaketon arrived in his highly polished police car.

'You can't park there, Sergeant.' I went across to him as he was positioning his car in the space reserved for the groom's parents. 'Those places are for the official cars. Guests are over there.' I pointed to a space on the edge of the moor. 'Could you go over there?' and I indicated a space about a hundred yards distant, far enough to be out of the way of incoming vehicles.

'Where's your van?' he demanded, not looking very pleased.

'At home, Sergeant,' I said. 'I left it to reduce the pressure on parking space.'

'And where will the chief constable be parking?' was his next question.

'He's one of the guests, he'll be over there,' and I indicated the areas I had earmarked.

'But surely his will be one of the official cars, Rhea....'

'No, Sergeant, they include the bride, the bridesmaids, the bride's parents, the groom's parents, immediate family....'

'I can't say I like that at all, Rhea, the chief constable being relegated to the status of an ordinary guest.'

'He is an ordinary guest, Sergeant; this is not an official engagement for him. There are some very important and high-ranking military officers here too, and they're also being treated as ordinary guests. I've discussed it with Mr Perry-Smith and neither the chief nor the army officers want preferential treatment from us; he stressed that. The day belongs to the bride and groom, not the chief constable!'

'Well, I can't say I agree with all that, Rhea, but it's their show,' and he drove away to park. I smiled to myself; that was one small victory for me.

Within minutes, the guests were arriving with increasing frequency and there was a flurry of activity as they parked, smartened their clothes, posed for photographs, kissed and renewed old acquaintance before eventually entering the church. The chief constable, his wife, son and daughter arrived and entered the fun of the moment before entering the church – Blaketon threw up a smart salute but the chief either did not see it or chose to ignore the sergeant. Blaketon seemed to be treading on hot-bricks – he could not keep still, although he did simmer down once the chief had entered the church. And then it was 3 p.m., everyone went inside, save the official photographer.

The bridal cars began to arrive; first the mother of the bride, then the bridesmaids and finally the bride beside her father in a splendid white Rolls Royce, hired for the occasion.

'Everything going all right?' called Mr Perry-Smith as he stood with his daughter on his arm, ready to make an entry.

'Fine,' I said. 'No problems at all.'

'Good, now for the important bit!' he grinned, kissing his daughter. 'Come on, Val, it's down to you now!'

And so they processed into the church. As the organ played the bride into the church, I said, 'I'm going to stand at the back, Sergeant, and watch her get married.'

'A good idea,' he said, joining me. And so, as the bride joined the groom before the altar, Sergeant Blaketon and I slid into the back of the church to enjoy the ceremonial. But one of the ushers spotted us.

'Bride or groom?' he grinned.

'Bride,' I said, showing my invitation.

And so we took our seats. As the music continued, Blaketon leaned over and said, 'Rhea, are you a guest?'

'Yes, Sergeant.' I showed him the official invittion. 'I'm invited to go to the reception.'

'Oh,' was all he said. 'And I take it you will not be

drinking on duty?'

'I have the chief constable's permission,' I said, hoping I was not telling an outright lie.

'Really?'

'He suggested I be invited to keep an eye on the presents, but to be a guest at the same time.'

'All I can say is don't make a fool of yourself, Rhea, remember you are in uniform.'

'Of course, Sergeant,' I smiled, as the organ ceased.

'Ladies and gentlemen,' began the vicar. 'We are gathered here before God and in the face of this congregation....'

Like all church weddings, it was a moving occasion and although it took about an hour, it seemed to be over far too quickly. I decided to dash outside ahead of the bride and groom, and left my seat as the final hymn was being sung; Blaketon followed but when we got outside, he said, 'God help me, Rhea! What's he doing here?'

Standing beside a rickety trestle-table full of empty beer glasses and jugs, which he'd erected near the lychgate, was none other than Claude Jeremiah Greengrass. There was some kind of calor gas cooker burning beneath the table and his filthy old truck was parked right outside the entrance. The smell he was producing was far from pleasant. With me trotting behind, Sergeant Blaketon galloped down the path, calling, 'Greengrass, get yourself and that awful vehicle of yours out of my sight before I have you arrested. And shift that table and whatever you've got on it. And under it.'

'I'm here officially, Sergeant,' beamed Claude. 'I'm fulfilling an ancient Aidensfield custom.'

'Not if I have anything to do with it, you're not!'

At that point, one of the ushers came out of the church and hurried to talk to Claude. 'Ah, you've made it, Mr Greengrass. Everything all right?'

'Apart from this daft copper trying to kick me out,' grinned Claude. 'For a bloke who's more ancient than a lot of my customs, he knows nowt about ancient customs, do you Sergeant Blaketon?'

'What's going on?' asked Sergeant Blaketon, and I must

admit I was beginning to wonder too.

'Bride ale, Sergeant.' Claude was enjoying this. 'I'm supplying bride ale to all the guests, in accordance with our custom.'

'You're not allowed to sell intoxicating liquor without a licence, Greengrass!' Blaketon was working himself into a very official mood now. 'And I'll have you know the chief constable is in that church, and if you think you can break the law on my patch before his very eyes....'

'Break what law?' chuckled Claude. 'I'm not breaking any law. I'm not selling the stuff. I'm giving it away, free, gratis and for nowt. It's my own brew, Greengrass's Home Brewed Barn Stormer, and I'm giving it away to all the guests. It has to be warmed up, you see, Sergeant, hot ale. That's what the heater's for.'

'I don't believe this!' grunted Blaketon. 'Rhea, you never briefed me about this performance.'

'I had no idea, Sergeant, but it's a bit like the bride kissing a chimney sweep, it brings good luck!'

'Greengrass bringing good luck? I'll never believe that, so help me!'

I now saw that Claude had a large cauldron below his table and it was full of a foul-looking brew; he swirled it with a massive wooden spoon as he grinned at the helpless Blaketon, saying, 'It has to be spiced an' all, so I've brought a few eastern promises along. There's bits of all sorts in this; it's t'best bride ale this side of the pyramids, Sergeant. By gum, with a drop of this stuff inside 'em, they'll have a whale of a time in that marquee, there'll be a fair bit of hair letting down tonight. You know, if this stuff's popular, I might patent the recipe. How about that for a money-making idea, eh? Home-brewed bride ale, suitable for all weddings, luckier than horseshoes and cleaner than chimney sweeps....'

'Rhea, can't we stop this?'

'It was Mr Perry-Smith's idea,' smiled the usher. 'A surprise for everyone. He cleared it with the chief constable first, of course, you know, the legality side of things. So, Mr Greengrass, when everyone emerges, you offer them a glass of your bride ale.'

Claude's brew was the hit of the day. I tasted some and it was surprisingly palatable, and soon everyone was milling around with a glass in their hands as the first batch of official photographs were being taken. Even Sergeant Blaketon consented to taste a drop and didn't spit it out and so the bride ale plan had been a successful surprise.

Then, as everyone was moving away to the reception, Mr Perry-Smith called to Claude,

'See you at the reception, Claude? Thanks for arranging this surprise.'

'Aye, right, thanks. I am a bit hungry and could just see off a bit of smoked salmon and caviare, washed down with the best chanpagne....'

'And you, PC Rhea.'

But Sergeant Blaketon, an attempted gatecrasher, had not been invited at the outset and, as we all made our way from the church, I felt rather sorry for him. But it was his own fault – he had no cause to impose himself upon the wedding. Then as the chief constable left the church, he went across and shook Blaketon's hand, saying, 'It all went very well, Sergeant, thank you for coming.' And that was that.

But as everyone was heading for the marquee, Mrs Perry-Smith noticed Blaketon.

'I'll send a piece of wedding cake to the police station,' she called after him.

The financing of an Anglican parish church is a complex affair, with rules governing the use of monies collected in church and more rules governing monies collected outside the church which are destined for 'church purposes'. Over and above such rules, there is a common-law duty of the parishioners to maintain their parish church in repair which means they are ultimately liable to provide the funds necessary to keep the fabric of the church in proper repair.

The precise interpretation of this provision has been questioned; in my time at Aidensfield, nothing in the Compulsory Church Rate Abolition Act of 1868 or in the Parochial Church Councils (Powers) Measure of 1921 altered that duty. It was in 1921, however, that the duties and liabilities of the churchwardens relating to the care, maintenance, preservation and insurance of the fabric of the church were transferred to the parochial church council; nonetheless, it remained the duty of the parishioners to repair their parish church.

One exception was the chancel – in this case, the responsibility for repairs rested with the rector, unless there was a custom for the parishioners to repair it. And it was that custom which led to a problem at Aidensfield. In the case of Aidensfield, it seemed that Henry VIII, prior to creating his Church of England and making himself head of the church instead of the pope, had enshrined that custom in the form of a written order. In simple terms, it said that people living in the parish of Aidensfield were responsible for repairs to the chancel of their parish church. The effect of this was, of course, to make the parishioners responsible for the entire building – on the face of things, a sensible notion.

Over the years, collections had been made on a regular basis and most of the necessary work had been undertaken. The church seemed to be in good repair. But apparently there had been problems with the chancel for some years; precisely what those problems were had never been made public but money had been raised by the parishioners and used for work that was, in effect, little more than a cosmetic exercise.

It had involved superficial repairs such as filling in cracks and painting them over or treating any dampness with modern cover-up methods. The new vicar, the Reverend Christian Lord, sensed that something more serious was wrong and that the underlying problem had never been identified. As a consequence, he decided to arrange a thorough examination of the building by experts. It was then discovered that the ancient wooden beams beneath the floor of the chancel were rotten. Over many decades, water had seeped into the foundations and the thick supporting beams were like soggy blotting paper – urgent and major repairs were needed. The task of removing everything from the chancel, including the altar, was daunting, but if the floor was to be repaired and sealed to prevent a repetition, it had to be done. There was no alternative. The next stage was to determine the cost. The first all-inclusive estimate came to a staggering £95,000.

It was then that The Revd Lord settled down to examine ways of raising the money; officially designated the rector of Aidensfield, he came across the old law that the rector was responsible for the upkeep of the chancel, except in the case of Aidensfield where it appeared to rest with the parishioners. But on reading the rule carefully, the wording did not say 'parishioners', it said that *people living within the parish of Aidensfield* were responsible for the chancel – and that included everyone, not merely those who attended the Anglican church. According to that wording, it included Catholics, Methodists, Quakers, non-Christians – the lot. Furthermore, it said that the constable was responsible for collecting the money!

Armed with this discovery, Christian Lord asked if I would mind popping in to have a chat with him – he said it would be better done at the rectory because all the relevant papers were too many to carry with him. I agreed. After explaining his discovery, he said, 'I realize this has nothing to do with the police, Nick, but as the constable is mentioned in the statute, I thought you had better be told. It looks as though you have to go around and gather the money.' He looked worried as he imparted this piece of information.

At that stage, however, he did not tell me how much money was required.

'You can't be serious, Christian!' I cried. 'That reference is to the old parish constables of centuries ago, not the modern policeman.'

'It's all written down here, Nick. "It shall be the duty of the constable of Aidensfield to collect the monies". It's all here, in black-and-white. You are the constable.'

'But it's not part of a policeman's duties to go around collecting dues for the established church, Christian. Those days have long gone – you need an official collection agent, someone appointed especially to undertake that duty.'

'The whole thing's going to cause an immense fuss,' he

said. 'Look, do you know how many regular parishioners I have?'

'No idea,' I shook my head. 'I'm a Catholic, I go to my own church.'

'Sixty at the outside. Twenty regulars, the others mainly at Christmas and Easter. Now, if I ask them to pay for those repairs ...'

'Which is their statutory duty!' I smiled.

'And which will cost £95,000,' he grimaced.

'How much?' I almost shouted.

He repeated the figure. I did a rapid piece of mental arithmetic and worked out that each of his parishioners had to find around £1583 – some three or four years' wages for the average person living on these moors. It was then that he revealed that the wording referred to all the people living within the parish, rather than those who attended the Anglican church. That would considerably reduce individual payments, but I said, 'But, Christian, you can't make them pay! There's non-Christians, Catholics, Quakers and others.'

'There is provision for us to seek a court order to compel payments.' He hung his head as he uttered those words. 'Things were harsh in the days of Henry VIII!'

'Don't I know it!' The aftermath of Henry's actions led to two or three bleak centuries for Catholics in England with executions and confiscation of their lands and property. 'Look, if the people of the village were asked to give money, or attend a fund-raising event or buy raffle tickets, they'd support your case, but you can't go *demanding* money from them. I know the Catholics would support you – they want the church to be in good condition when it's returned to them!' It was an old comment, often used, and I couldn't resist it. 'So how many people live in the parish of Aidensfield?'

'Four hundred and fifty in round terms,' he said. 'There are two hundred and fifty houses in the parish.'

'So if every household was asked to pay the cost, each paying the same amount, you'd be asking £380 from every house. Slightly less than a year's wages for some of our local people. That's a crippling demand, Christian. You can't do it, it's evil.'

'I have no alternative,' he said slowly. 'None at all.'

'You mean you are going ahead? But I refuse to knock on people's doors, as a village policeman, to collect debts of that kind. I cannot do it. It's not part of my official duties, and I won't do it when I'm off duty either!'

'I knew you could not accept, but I had to ask. I will now send a letter to everyone in the village to put my case. And then I'll await the flack!' he grimaced.

'You know you'll never get money by using those tactics!' I wondered why he was smiling.

'But I will get publicity.' He smiled now. 'Someone is bound to inform the newspapers and the publicity might jerk the Church Commissioners and the diocese into doing something ... they're dragging their heels at the moment. No one wants to know about our problems.'

The Reverend Lord did send his letter and the accompanying demand for £380 per household to everyone living in Aidensfield and it produced a furious response. Some even went to the rectory to vent their anger by hammering on the door and shouting abuse, others just ignored it, many felt it was nothing to do with them and some didn't even open the letter, thinking it was a circular of some kind. But his ruse worked.

One of the recipients rang the *Daily Mail* and within days a reporter and photographer had arrived and the story made national news. There were photographs of the chancel, as yet untouched by the workmen, quotes from the experts who had discovered the cause of the problem and before too long, the village of Aidensfield was featured on television, radio and in other papers, both local and national.

One result was unexpected – people who had read about the dilemma facing the parish sent in donations; small cheques and postal orders flooded into the rectory. One man sent a cheque for £3,000 saying his ancestors were buried in Aidensfield and he loved the church; a national newspaper organized its own appeal; people in the vicinity offered to organize money-raising events ranging from concerts to guessing the weight of pigs and the village rallied to the support of the Revd Lord. Thanks to the publicity, £19,000 had been raised or promised within a week, an astonishing sum, but it was enough for the authorities to give the go-ahead for the work to begin.

And I did not have to traipse around the village to collect the money! But when the work started, it meant that services could not be held in the church and so the Catholics offered their building to the Anglicans until the repairs were finished.

'And,' said Father Adrian, the Catholic priest, at mass before the Anglicans arrived for their first service, 'whilst they are using our church, we shall give them half our profits from bingo to be used for repairs to their chancel. After all, we do want the church to be in good condition when it is restored to us.'

'Amen,' said someone in the congregation.

Today, the chancel of Aidensfield Parish Church is sound and in a state of excellent repair. Most of the money was raised within eighteen months, and I believe the balance was finally paid ten years later, thanks to an on-going series of raffles, whist drives and other money-raising events – plus a continuing sum from the Catholics' bingo sessions.

But that old custom concerning repairs to the chancel remains in force. Perhaps a village constable in the year 2464 will be asked to help to collect the funds again and I wonder what the reaction of that community will be?

4

'I was found of them that sought me not.'

Rom. 10.20

Turkeys are usually associated with Christmas dinner but I remember, some years ago, a campaign was launched by turkey farmers to persuade people to eat turkey at other times of the year. Easter was one of the suggested occasions, this being recommended as a good turkey-eating time due to the celebratory nature of that popular Christian festival but the real hope was that we would eat turkey all the year round. After all, there is no reason to restrict the eating of turkey to the Christmas holiday or to any other festive occasion.

It was a Yorkshireman, William Strickland of Boynton in the East Riding, who introduced turkeys to this country. Contrary to popular belief, these birds do not come from Turkey, but from South America. It was while sailing with Sebastian Cabot that Strickland found himself in charge of a ship which carried a few strange-looking birds from America back to England. These were quickly and easily sold for fourpence each, a high price at the time. Strickland realized that these quaint creatures might find a wider sale and so he developed the importation of turkeys to such an extent that he was soon chartering his own ship to bring them into Britain. Such was the success of his venture, that he bought Boynton Hall near Bridlington, became the squire in 1549 and was knighted. George II gave his approval to this new-found meat and eventually the royal park at Richmond became a thriving turkey farm, producing some 3000 birds for the royal palate.

Even today, some of the largest producers of turkeys are in East Yorkshire, with the British consuming more than seventeen million turkeys every year. In spite of continuing attempts to convince us they are excellent at any time of the year, most are consumed at Christmas.

Whilst appreciating their popularity, I must admit I was surprised to find a turkey in the outbuilding which was attached to my police house at Aidensfield. It was a few days before Easter and I was enjoying my days off, on this occasion a Saturday and Sunday together, a rare treat. With the children, Mary and I had been shopping on the Saturday morning and after lunch in a local café, we returned home. I was hoping to tidy the garden that same afternoon because my parents and my in-laws were coming for lunch on Sunday. I wanted the place to look as neat as possible and so there was a lot of preparation on the Saturday – my task was to make the garden look presentable after the winter neglect while Mary concentrated upon the house.

Determined to tackle the worst of the rubbish, I went into the outhouse to seek my gardening tools. There was no door on this outhouse – it was part of a passage which extended the width of the property between the house and the garage. The builders had produced a small cave-like structure which could accommodate things like the lawnmower, spade and a selection of hoes. It was always open, the through-passage sheltering the outhouse entrance from the worst of the weather. But anyone could walk into that outbuilding. Thus I went in to get my gardening tools and there, on a battered old table I used as a workbench, was a large cardboard box.

I hadn't left it there and it had not been there earlier that morning. Puzzled, I opened it and inside found a fresh turkey. It was dead and quite naked, having been expertly plucked and dressed. Beyond all doubt, it was ready for the oven.

Like all rural constables at that time, I knew that country people proffered their appreciation by giving village bobbies presents like pheasants, grouse, rabbits, hares, salmon and the like. In many cases, these items of game were dressed ready for the oven, but from time to time, such gifts needed plucking or dressing. In all cases, though, there was never any question of bribery or corruption – it was a simple way for country people to express their thanks for some past act of kindness by the constable. It was *not* for overlooking petty offences or a means of persuading us to close our eyes to some future breaches of the law. It was a thank-you – nothing less and nothing more.

But as I stared at the turkey, I could not reccall any incident which would have merited such a thank-you present. I could not recall performing any extra assistance in recent weeks to anyone on my patch. The turkey presented a puzzle, therefore, but a welcome one. I searched the interior of the box for a note, but there was none, neither was there a scribbled message on the walls of the box. Whoever had left this turkey did not wish to be known. It was an anonymous gift. I could only guess that it had arrived that morning while we were away from the house. It seemed very fresh and it had come at just the right time. Had I mentioned to anyone that Mary and I were entertaining our respective parents for lunch on Sunday?

I could not recall chatting to anyone about it during my rounds – but in the circumstances, the arrival of the turkey was extremely fortuitous. Puzzled but quite delighted, I carried my trophy into the kitchen and plonked it on the table; it must have weighed twelve pounds or more, and then I called Mary.

'I got a joint of beef for tomorrow,' she said upon inspecting the huge bird. 'But will that turkey go in the oven?' was her next thought.

She opened the door and, after a bit of squeezing into our largest roasting tin, she made sure the bird did fit the oven.

'I can keep the meat in the fridge; we can use it later in

the week,' she said. 'This bird will be fine, but needs cooking straight away. Who gave it to you?'

'I have no idea,' I explained. 'Have you done anyone a favour recently? Or mentioned tomorrow's family lunch?'

She could not think of anything she had done or any remark she had made which would have prompted its delivery. Furthermore, there were no turkey farms on my beat and so the gift had not come from a grateful businessman. As we puzzled for a long time over the reason for its anonymous arrival, neither of us could think of anyone who might have left us this tasty present. If there was a problem, though, it was that it had to be dealt with fairly soon. The joint of beef was small enough to be kept in the fridge for a later meal and so we could make good use of this gift. It was abundantly clear that someone had known we were having important guests and had wanted us to be in a position to celebrate to the full. A lovely gesture.

'Even if we don't know where it's come from, we'll make the most of it,' Mary beamed. 'We can have quite a party. It'll be like Christmas all over again.'

Our efforts on the Saturday afternoon made the house and garden presentable and the children grew quite excited at the prospect of having both sets of grandparents for lunch. Together, we prepared the vegetables and potatoes on Saturday evening, ready for Sunday, and then early on Sunday morning, Mary placed the huge turkey in the oven. It should be ready around one o'clock, we reckoned. After early mass, we returned home to finalize the arrangements, set the table, organize the sherry glasses and complete those countless chores which precede a visit of such importance to a family.

And then, around half past ten, there was a knock on the door. Groaning because it might mean work on my day off, I went to answer it and standing there was Father Adrian, the Catholic parish priest.

'Father Adrian!' I said, 'Come in.'

'I saw you at mass but you're not in uniform, Nick?' he observed. 'Does that mean you are not at work?'

He removed his black trilby and followed me into the

house. He was a Benedictine monk from Maddleskirk Abbey who served as the parish priest; an affable man, he was tall and stately with a round happy face and a mop of thick white hair. He sniffed the air in our entrance hall and smiled. 'Sunday lunch cooking, eh? What a lovely smell....'

'Yes, I have my parents coming, and my in-laws,' I told him. 'They live fairly close together and will be coming in the same car. It's nice when they can share lifts like that.'

'I do enjoy family occasions,' he smiled. 'We have a lovely community at the abbey but we do lack a sense of family, mother, father, children, grandparents – all that.'

'So what can I do for you?.' I asked him.

'I've come to report a theft, Nick,' he said. 'But if you're not on duty....'

'I can have one of my colleagues from Ashfordly come and deal with it,' I said. 'It's no trouble. I'll ring straight away. But a theft? Not from the church, surely?'

I wondered if I had a case of sacrilege on my patch! In those days, sacrilege was a very serious crime, equal to robbery and burglary in the severity of its sentence and the occurrence of it on my beat would cause Sergeant Blaketon to reach for his indigestion tablets. It was committed when someone broke into a church and stole anything at all.

'Well, I think it might be theft, it's the only answer to a riddle,' he said. 'It's disappeared from the doorstep outside the church.'

'What has?' I asked.

'A turkey,' he said, and my heart sank. 'Uncooked, but ready for the oven.'

'You'd better come into the office,' I said, shouting to Mary. 'Mary? Can we fix two cups of coffee?'

He settled on a chair beside my desk and I asked, 'Father, this turkey. Tell me about it.'

'I had arranged for several of my more elderly and lonely parishioners to have lunch together today,' he said. 'We are going to use Sybil McDonald's house – she has the space you see, there's half a dozen of them, that's all. It's nice for pensioners to have companionship, especially on a Sunday. So the idea was that the cooks at the abbey would put the turkey in the oven while doing the normal lunch, and I would collect it when it was ready. It's only a two-minute drive from the abbey to Sybil's house, you see, it would keep nice and hot on the short trip.'

'Have you asked at the abbey?'

'Well, yes, that's the point. I was called away yesterday, unexpectedly, but had arranged for the butcher to leave the turkey with me at the church. I had intended to be there all day Saturday, you see, and would have taken the turkey along to the abbey when I had finished at St Aidan's.'

'So you were not there when the butcher arrived at the church?'

'Exactly, Nick.'

'And the butcher left the turkey at the church door? On the step outside?'

'Yes.'

That meant we were not talking about a case of sacrilege and, with some relief, I asked the priest to continue.

'I rang him this morning when I couldn't trace it. He assures me he left it in a cardboard box on the step of the church, nicely out of sight from the street. Now, Nick, when I came back yesterday evening, there was no turkey on the step.'

'And you therefore assumed someone had taken it along to the abbey to be cooked today?'

'Well, yes, I did. Sybil knew the arrangements – she's cooking the vegetables because the turkey's too large for her modest oven. Several helpers knew about the arrangements too. So naturally, when I didn't find the turkey last night, I assumed someone had come across it and dealt with it.'

I was growing more and more embarrassed as the story unfolded and could see myself being arrested for receiving stolen property even if there was no crime of sacrilege. I was now sure that Father Adrian's turkey was cooking beautifully in my oven.

'And when did you realize it hadn't arrived at the abbey?'

'Not long ago, Nick. I went back to the abbey after mass and popped into the kitchens to check that the system was working, but was told that the turkey hadn't arrived. We made a thorough search of the kitchens and any other place it might have been placed, but it never arrived at the abbey, Nick, and none of the helpers has seen it. Yet the butcher swears he placed it on the threshold of the church doorway yesterday evening, about six o'clock, he says.'

'Father,' I said. 'Bless me, for I have sinned ... I think I have a confession to make.'

'Well, Nick, come and see me at the church.' And then he realized what I was trying to say. 'Is that a turkey cooking in your kitchen?' he smiled.

'It is,' I nodded, and then explained what had happened.

He listened intently as I made my explanation, then asked, 'But who would put it in your outhouse?'

'I have no idea,' I admitted. 'But after what you have told me, I think someone, not knowing about your plans, found the box on the church step and brought it here for safe-keeping. We were away for a while, you see, so it was left in the outhouse. There was no note, and we've had no telephone calls about it, nothing to explain its presence. Naturally, I thought it was a gift.'

'Oh dear,' he said. 'What a mix-up!'

'Look,' I said. 'We can't let those poor old folks go without their dinner, Father, I know how they look forward to this kind of thing. If Sybil is cooking the vegetables, you can tell them we are cooking the turkey. I'll bring it down to Sybil's when it's cooked, about one o'clock. Then your problem is solved!'

'But yours isn't,' he said. 'You have guests due at almost any time and if you give me the turkey, you'll have nothing.'

'We have a joint of beef,' I said. 'Mary bought it yesterday before we found the turkey. We can pop it in the oven the minute the turkey's removed, and have a late lunch. An hour or so is neither here nor there....'

'Well, actually, there may be a better solution. When I failed to locate the turkey, I did make contingency plans,' he said. 'I asked the abbot if the abbey would supply the meat for today's lunch, and I have a car standing by to drive a joint of beef down to us when it's ready.'

At that stage, Mary entered with the two mugs of coffee, and I explained things to her; like me, she blushed crimson at the thought of the village policeman and his family tucking into a stolen turkey and when I said I would take the cooked bird down to Sybil's she agreed wholeheartedly.

'It'll be nice to do something for them,' she blushed. 'Yes, Nick, do that. Consider it done, Father.'

'Nick,' he sipped from his coffee. 'As I told you, I do have a secondary supply of food coming from the abbey kitchens ... I merely came here to report a theft, not to cadge food. Things have changed somewhat!'

'Our parents will not mind one iota,' I said.

'Look, the idea of getting these pensioners – parishioners and pensioners they are – together on a Sunday is to give them something to talk about, something of interest, so why don't you and all your family come and join us? Sybil's house is large enough for us all and you could help us eat both the turkey and the beef brought from the abbey. There'll be more than enough for my purpose.'

Mary looked at me and smiled.

'I think my mum and dad would like that,' she said. 'They love meeting new people to swap yarns with.'

'And hasn't Sybil got a collection of toys and dolls' houses?' I recalled, wondering how my children were going to occupy themselves.

'She has,' smiled Father Adrian. 'So leave it with me. Give me time to alert Sybil and I'll see you all at her house at one o'clock!'

It was a lovely occasion, with our parents, children and the pensioners of the parish of St Aidan's, Aidensfield, having a most enjoyable lunch. As I tucked into the turkey I could hear Mary's dad explaining the history of the railway which ran through the village. Sybil had some paintings of railway engines on her dining-room walls and it was clear that my father-in-law was thoroughly enjoying

himself, as were the others. Mother-in-law had found a
lady who shared her interest in gardening while my
mother's knowledge of history was tested by a lady who
had lectured in history at university. My dad was content
to talk about fishing to a gentleman who had been a water
bailiff while the children were captivated by Sybil's
collection of toys. Mary and I did enjoy the outing, even
though I was momentarily reminded of the old saying.
'Stollen meate is sweetest'.

But I never did discover who had placed that turkey in
my outhouse.

The turkey wasn't the only problem at the doorstep of St
Aidan's Catholic Church in Aidensfield. A far more
serious problem was discovered by the church cleaner,
Bernadette O'Hara, an Irish-born lady of some sixty-two
summers and no husbands. Known to the village as Miss
Bernadette, she followed a nun-like existence in a tiny
cottage with the church as her sole interest (or was it soul
interest?).

Always dressed in dark blue dresses, sensible black
shoes, black stockings and a dark headscarf, she looked
like a nun, although she had been a secretary in her early
life. Devoted to the church in both the spiritual and
practical sense, Miss Bernadette unlocked the doors at 7
a.m. in time for daily mass at 7.30 a.m.; on most mornings,
she flitted around the church, dusting the statues of The
Sacred Heart, Our Lady and St Aidan or polishing the altar
rails before the arrival of Father Adrian and his devoted
congregation. He had a good congregation at his daily
masses, people preferring to begin their day at work with
a prayer. On Sundays, Feast Days and Holy Days of
Obligation Bernadette opened the doors at 6.30 a.m. for a
more prolonged bout of dusting and polishing prior to
those masses and, because she hated getting out of bed
early in the day, she regarded her efforts as a sacrifice to
God himself, as well as to Jesus, Mary and Joseph. There is
little doubt that Miss Bernadette felt that her devotions
would send her soul soaring straight to Heaven when God
was ready to carry her from this mortal life – and I

wondered if she would polish the pearly gates as well as she tended St Aidan's. I felt sure she would happily polish them for eternity, just in case there was something better in the future.

On Thursday, 18 August, she rose from her slumbers at 6 a.m., said her morning prayers, got dressed and pottered up to the church in time to open the doors at 6.30 a.m., this being the Feast Day of St Helen. Mass was at 7.30 a.m. and she expected a congregation of about a dozen, several of whom would be called Helen, like Helen Grieveson and Helen Jones. But when she arrived, there was a package on the step of the church.

It was right outside the door so that anyone wishing to enter would have to step over it. On closer examination, she realized it was more than a package, it was a carry cot. It was a blue one made of plastic, with a hood in the raised position and carrying-handles at either side.

Thinking that one of the local Helens had arrived early for mass and placed it there temporarily, Miss Bernadette looked into the cot and found it contained a very young but blissfully contented baby, fast asleep. It was probably a girl because the clothes and covers were all pink. Miss Bernadette tried the door of the church, but it was locked, so the mother was not inside. Maybe she was wandering around the outside of the church, looking at the stained-glass windows or something? Passing away the time until mass started.

'Hello, is anyone there?' Miss Bernadette called in vain. She pottered around the external portions of the church, hoping she might find someone who was responsible for the child, but there was nobody. The church and its surrounds, including the entire village main street, were deserted. There were no cars in the car-park, no people to be seen. Miss Bernadette was alone with the baby. It took a few minutes for her to realize that there was a distinct possibility that this baby had been abandoned.

'Holy Mother of God,' she whispered to herself, looking down at the peaceful babe. 'Who could do such a thing?'

Even at this late stage, she felt that the parents, the mother at least, would come rushing towards her with some excuse such as 'I'm sorry, I had nowhere else to put her', or 'I had to dash to find a toilet', or 'I'm looking for Rose Cottage', but there was nothing. No one came. Miss Bernadette made the sign of the cross, said a quick Hail Mary and decided she must do something fairly quickly – so she unlocked the door of the church, took the carry-cot inside and placed it on the front pew, right before the altar. The tiny child, only a day or so old, slept through all this initial activity.

Miss Bernadette thought that if the mother did arrive to claim the child, she would surely come into the church and besides, Father Adrian would be here just after seven. She would ask his advice. He would know what to do. And suppose the mother never returned? Had the child been baptized? Maybe the first thing the priest should do is to baptize the baby....

These thoughts ranged through her head as she dusted and polished, stopping every few minutes to peep at the sleeping child. Very shortly afterwards, the congregation began to arrive. Miss Bernadette thought it best not to mention the baby at this stage; Father Adrian should be the first to know. By 6.15, several men and women, including two Helens, had arrived and taken their seats, none occupying the front pew and so the baby slept on, undisturbed and unnoticed. Then Father Adrian, a monk who lived in the monastry at Maddleskirk Abbey, came rushing in, slightly out of breath and said to Miss Bernadette, 'Sorry I am later than usual, the car wouldn't start,' and he rushed into the vestry to don his robes. He would still be able to commence mass on time; the people wanted that because some had to get to work.

Miss Bernadette followed him into the vestry.

'Father,' she said quietly, closing the door behind herself, 'I have something to tell you.'

'Can it wait until after mass?' he smiled.

'No.' She was firm, even though she was speaking to a priest. 'No, it cannot. I fear we have been left a baby, a very tiny one,' and she told her story.

'It's here you mean? In church?' He was horrified.

'I have not told anyone else,' she said confidentially. 'I

was not sure what we should do.'

'I will pray for the child at mass,' was his first response. 'But surely a mother can't abandon a child like this? Could she just dump it on a church doorstep?'

'I fear some can, Father.' Miss Bernadette had read of such happenings. 'Now, it will need feeding sooner or later, and it might wake up and cry and we have to decide what to do about it.'

'Well, I shall say mass first, that will give the mother time to contact us if she wants to, and then we will have to contact the police. I am sure they have a system for dealing with abandoned babies.'

And that is what they did. Father Adrian said a short mass, lasting only some twenty minutes in case the child awoke and began to cry, and then, when the congregation had departed, he carried out an emergency baptism upon the baby with Miss Bernadette acting as godparent. They called her Helen after the saint whose feast day they were celebrating, and adding 'Aidensfield' as a surname.

Shortly afterwards, he and Miss Bernadette arrived at my house in his car, complete with the carry-cot and its sad contents. I had just clambered out of bed after working a late shift the previous night, and we were in the midst of trying to get the children out of bed and dressed, even if it was in the middle of school holidays. Mary was intending to take them to visit one of her sisters today.

'Say that again, Father?' I peered into the carry-cot which was now lying on my desk in the office with the baby fast asleep.

He and Miss Bernadette told their story and I could not believe it.

'But surely the mother must have intended to return?' I put to Miss Bernadette. 'She's probably frantic by now, looking for her child!'

'The child was there at half past six this morning,' said Miss Bernadette. 'On the doorstep. I took her into the church and it's now after eight o'clock … with no sign of the mother. She's had plenty of time to return to the church and take her baby back, but she hasn't. So what shall we do, Constable?'

'Mary!' I opened the door of my office and called my wife.

'I brought her here because I knew you were a family man,' said the priest. 'You and your wife know how to deal with babies.'

'Who's this?' Mary smiled as she peered into the cot. We stood around in shocked silence and told Mary the sad story. Tears misted across her eyes as she tenderly lifted the tiny child out of the carry-cot. Its eyes were open now, but it was not crying. 'I don't believe it, how could anyone do this ... come along, you'll soon want something to eat ... I hope I have something that will do....'

'Hang on,' I said. As Mary had disturbed the coverlets, it revealed at the foot of the cot, hidden beneath the blankets, an envelope, some extra nappies, spare clothes and a baby's bottle full of milk.

'It'll need warming.' Having borne four children of her own, Mary knew exactly what to do and carried the now crying child into the house, along with the bottle. 'She'll need feed every four hours. You found her at half-past six, Miss Bernadette?'

'I did, sure as I am here.'

'So if the tiny mite was fed at five o'clock or just afterwards, she'll soon need another feed. I'll see to that.'

Soon, the child would have its nappy changed and it would be fed if and when Mary considered it necessary. With the baby gone, I opened the envelope. On pink paper there was scribbled a pencilled note which said, *Whoever finds her, please look after her. And please baptize her.*

And that was all – except we now knew for certain it was a girl.

'I have baptized her, Nick, it was an emergency baptism in light of the unusual circumstances. I called her Helen Aidensfield but if her parents do turn up, they might want something else on her birth certificate. You'll know what to do next?' Father Adrian put to me.

'I've never dealt with an abandoned baby before,' I had to admit. 'But I am sure there are procedures. First, we need to find the mother, she's obviously a Catholic who understands the need for baptism, but she's clearly in need of help, either medical or psychological or both.'

'I don't think she's a local girl,' said the priest. 'I am sure I would have known if any of my congregation or their relations had given birth or were about to.'

'I can have words with the doctors, midwives and local hospitals,' I said. 'We might be able to trace the mother through them.'

'She's only a day or two old, but well cared for, Constable,' said Miss Bernadette. 'The clothing is clean and of a very good quality.'

'If the mother is not from this area, it seems someone has deliberately chosen to leave the child on your church doorstep, Father; they must have travelled through the village by car. But why this particular church?'

'I can only suggest it's because it's a Catholic church. It reminds me of bygone times. Not long ago, when a Catholic mother gave birth to an illegitimate child and wanted to conceal the birth, she gave the child to a convent to be brought up and schooled. The shame of illegitimacy made them – and their parents – very secretive and irrational. Maybe there's a hint of that kind of thinking in this mother's behaviour?'

'She wants her child baptized a Catholic and brought up in a convent? You think that's the reason for all this? If so, this mother is not setting a very holy example to her baby daughter!' I commented.

'We must not condemn the mother,' said Father Adrian. 'We do not know what her motives were nor do we know what problems she was facing herself, possibly alone and with no one to guide her and no one to turn to for help.'

'She might be suffering from the effects of childbirth.' I was thinking of the crime of infanticide, committed by women whose state of mind had been adversely affected by giving birth.

'Very likely,' he said. 'But I wonder if she went to her own priest at any stage? Probably not but clearly she is in a very desperate state. But sadly, for the infant, there are better ways for starting one's life,' he added. 'To grow up unwanted must be a terrible cross to bear.'

I had to tackle this from a practical aspect. 'The point is, what do we do now? Clearly, the baby is in need of professional care.'

'Nazareth House in Middlesbrough cares for orphans,' he said. 'I will telephone them to see if they will admit this child.'

'And we will establish enquiries to trace the mother,' I said.

'Should she be found, will she be prosecuted?' asked Father Adrian.

'It is a crime to abandon or expose any child under two years of age whereby its life is endangered or its health is, or is likely to be permanently injured,' I quoted from the Offences Against the Person Act of 1861 still in force. 'An action of this kind is also regarded as cruelty to children, so the mother, or whoever placed the child on your doorstep, could be prosecuted under two statutes, but in practice, the courts take a lenient view of such behviour. Bearing in mind the problems faced by some new mothers, they do believe that treatment is more important than punishment.'

'You said "whoever placed the child there",' observed Father Adrian. 'You are not limiting that action to the mother?'

'Some stern fathers in these moorland areas have been known to take illegitimate babies away from their daughters,' I said. 'I was brought up around here, remember, and in Catholic eyes, I know it is still considered shameful to produce an illegitimate baby. Quite often in the past, the poor mothers of bairns born out of wedlock had no choice – their child was taken away and put in a home, a convent as a rule, with no questions asked. They thought it helped to preserve family dignity.'

'Sadly, I remember that kind of thing,' admitted Father Adrian. 'A cruel solution. And you think this might have happened here?'

'It's not impossible, Father,' I put to him. 'Think of the time the baby was left – the very early hours of the morning – and a car must have been used. How many young mums would have a car? And the condition of the clothing, the state of the carry-cot – it's all good quality material. This is no down-and-out youngster, Father, this is no young mum on the dole. The baby is very young too, a day old, two days at the most. It's been disposed of as soon as possible, so that no one has seen it with its new mother. A rapid disposal also means the mother has had no time to get attached to the child. This was a deliberate plan of action carried out with some forethought. I wouldn't be surprised if some Victorian type of parent had done this.'

'There are several people around here whose daughters are away from home, either working or at university,' he spoke gently and with a lot of thought.

'Precisely,' I said. 'So perhaps we are seeking a stern father as the person who abandoned the child? But whatever has happened, there will be a very unhappy young mother somewhere in the background.'

'And what will she be doing now?' he put to me.

'It wouldn't surprise me if she'd been sent away from home, to get over it, to an aunt or friend or someone similar. She'll be in hiding, at the behest of her family – that's my guess,' I said.

'There are times it's hard to love all the human race,' mused Father Adrian. 'So will the newspapers find out?'

'If we start asking questions around hospitals and surgeries, they might find out,' I said. 'But sometimes a feature in the newspaper is the only way to trace the mother. We might have to approach them to ask for news coverage. Readers may realize that a woman they saw with a baby two or three days ago, no longer has the child … so they'll ask themselves where's it gone? And where did this lovely blue carry-cot come from? It looks new, the shop might remember selling it or friends of the family might recall it. So in all sorts of ways, the newspapers can help us trace the mother – and don't forget she might want to be found,' I reminded them. 'She must be suffering terribly right now; we must not ignore her torment, Father, and we shall not. She might be depending upon the papers, radio or television to tell her what's happened to her child. But if the mother's parents have done this, the girl might have given birth at a hospital a long way from here. Questions asked locally might not produce any information whereas items in the national papers might produce a result for us.'

'Yes, well, you know your job,' he said. 'Look, I must be going. I will ring the nuns at Nazareth House in Middlesbrough straight away to see if they will take the child, at least on a temporary basis, and I will call you.'

'Shall I stay with you to help care for the child?' asked Miss Bernadette, clearly wishing to have some responsibility for her discovery.

'I'll let you speak to my wife about that,' I told her. 'You and Mary can decide what to do in the immediate future while I set the offical wheels in motion. Now, would you like to have a baptismal breakfast with us and your new god-daughter, Miss Bernadette?'

We had not yet had our breakfasts, and I knew that Miss Bernadette would not have eaten before Holy Communion, and so we all settled down for a celebratory meal of boiled eggs with soldiers, marmalade and toast and a pot of coffee. Baby Helen slept through what was probably her first and last family meal, and then Father Adrian rang to say that Nazareth House would accept the child, at least on a temporary basis. There was an enormous relief, even though Mary was already talking emotionally about adoption of the foundling; our children thought the baby was beautiful, which she was, and they wanted to keep her. But it wasn't quite so simple as that – for one thing, the distraught mother could arrive at any moment. Having fortified myself with a good breakfast, it was with very mixed feelings that I rang Sergeant Blaketon to decide the next course of action and set all kinds of official wheels in motion.

'Trace the mother and have her prosecuted for abandoning the child,' was his first reaction.

'Easier said than done, Sergeant,' I said. 'But I will commence enquiries straight away. It's the baby that concerns me....'

'The child will go to a place of safety, Rhea. Hospital surgery, remand home, police station or other suitable place, the occupier of which is willingly temporarily to receive an infant.' He was quoting direct from the

Children and Young Persons Act of 1933. 'Those are the places listed, or of course, it includes any home provided by the local authority.'

I suggested Nazareth House and gave my reasons; he agreed and I said Mary was prepared to drive the child to Middlesbrough, along with the baby's godmother.

'Godmother?' he echoed down the telephone. 'I thought the child had no known parents?'

'She was baptized this morning, Sergeant,' and I attempted to explain the Catholic procedure in such an emergency.

'Well, you'll know more than me about such things,' he said. 'All right, have the child taken to Nazareth House and set about tracing the mother. Circulate all police stations locally, and ask for enquiries to be made at hospitals, surgeries and the like. Get our photographic unit to take a picture of the baby and the carry-cot, and the bottle and other stuff that was placed inside. Then we'll get the newspapers and radio stations to do a story. It might help if we can get the child shown on television. That could persuade the mother to come forward.'

It was a frantic day. A local freelance photographer came to take the newspaper photographs and a reporter interviewed me and my family, Miss Bernadette and Father Adrian. Later, a TV news crew turned up and spent hours filming in and around the village, along with interviews of local churchgoers and early-morning workers. Then, as Mary, Miss Bernadette and my children set out upon their tearful journey to Nazareth House, I began to ask questions of doctors, midwives, surgeries, cottage hospitals and other likely places within a ten-mile radius of Aidensfield. I started with telephone enquiries but knew that in many cases, a personal visit would be necessary. And so the attempt to find the mother or even the grandparents of Baby Helen began in earnest.

All the local newspapers and regional TV programmes published the story with appealing pictures of Baby Helen and details of her meagre belongings. Radio stations carried the story too, and every hospital and other place likely to treat a pregnant, or recently pregnant woman, was visited either by me or by other police officers. But we never discovered anything that would lead us to the family or mother of Baby Helen.

Meanwhile, Baby Helen was thriving at Nazareth House; once word got around Aidensfield Miss Bernadette and other people from the village would regularly travel to Middlesbrough to visit the baby, as did Mary and I, along with our family. In some ways, Baby Helen was adopted by the villagers of Aidensfield, Catholics and non-Catholics alike.

The weeks rolled by; summer turned into autumn and some of the newspapers produced a follow-up story about Baby Helen's progress, but nothing that anyone did produced a name for the mother nor any clues about Helen's unknown ancestors. From time to time, Sergeant Blaketon nudged me and my colleagues at Ashfordly police station into renewing our unproductive enquiries but we discovered absolutely nothing. I was sure that Helen had been born a long way from Aidensfield, hence our lack of success, but I was equally sure that her mother – and grandparents – had some links with the village.

I did discover the names of several young women whose parents lived in the village, and who were working or living away from home, but in spite of some very discreet enquiries, could not prove that any of them had either been pregnant or had given birth. It was a most frustrating time and it became increasingly clear that whoever had engineered this cover-up of a birth had done so with considerable skill and cunning. Every trail we discovered ended in nothing. Baby Helen seemed destined to grow into a young woman who would never know her mother, father or family origins.

I was beginning to think we would never trace the mother but as Christmas approached, my hopes were increased. One of my parish duties was to help decorate St Aidan's for Christmas and, one afternoon in early December when I was off duty, I decided to pop into the church to measure the distances between various points to which I could attach any decorations. But when I went into the church, I saw that someone was kneeling in prayer before the crib at the side of the altar.

The crib contained statues of the baby Jesus lying in a manger with his parents alongside with the three wise men and animals looking on. I said nothing as I went about my own mission, making as little noise as I could, and then, in the silence of the church, I realized it was a young woman and that she was crying. I felt as if I was intruding upon her grief and made to leave, but she heard me. Rather hurriedly and looking somewhat embarrassed, she rose to her feet and dabbed at her eyes, then managed a weak smile.

'I'm sorry,' she said, sniffing back her tears in the hallowed silence of the church. 'I had no idea you were there....'

'Please, I was intruding....' I was not in uniform so she probably had no idea I was the local bobby. 'I came to measure up for the Christmas decorations.'

'Don't let me stop you,' she said. 'I was going anyway.'

'Are you all right?' I asked. 'Do you need help?'

'You're not the priest, are you?' her eyes were moist as she fought to control her emotions.

'No, I'm not, but if you need one, you can contact them at the abbey.'

'No, it's all right. I'll be fine. I must go now. Dad will be wondering where I've got to.'

And she left. I watched her go down the path but there was no car in the park; she turned right and strode away. It was some time before I realized she was the daughter of Jack and Maisie Haynes of Toft Farm, Elsinby.

Shortly after my arrival in Aidensfield, I'd seen them dropping her off at the bus stop in the village when she was at school; she'd caught the school bus from there. She'd be sixteen or seventeen then; now, she'd be in her early twenties. Although she had matured I could still recognize her. Afterwards, I made some very discreet enquiries about the girl – Cecilia – and learned she was at college in Manchester. Currently, she was at home for Christmas and, I was later to discover, her mother had been a nurse prior to her own marriage ... so could the girl have given birth at home?

Without direct questioning, it would be impossible to find out – and Manchester City Police would not have the manpower to visit every likely hospital or surgery to see if a student had been attending for treatment, but the sight of her weeping over the child Jesus did make me ponder.

Years later, Helen Aidensfield called to see us. She was in her twenties and was about to go off to Newcastle University to study French; we had kept in touch over the years but when she walked into our lounge, she was the double of that girl crying at the crib in church. They were so alike it was unbelievable.

Today, many years later as I record this story, Helen is approaching her thirtieth birthday. She kept in touch with us and with Miss Bernadette who faithfully supported her over the years. Miss Bernadette is now approaching ninety years of age and still attends mass every day, she adores her only godchild who is now married with two children of her own, a boy and a girl. So Helen has a family of her own at last.

But sometimes I wonder if the secret of her birth lies in that old farmhouse at Elsinby where Jack Haynes ruled with Victorian fervour. But I can't ask Jack or his wife. Both died a few years ago – oddly enough, both on St Helen's Day although three years apart. Maisie went first, and Jack died a very lonely man.

I often wondered why his daughter never came to visit him.

5

'Thou shalt give the congregation and their beasts drink.'

Num. 20.8

'Nick, do you think the chief constable would give permission for a police dog to come to Aidensfield church?'

The Reverend Christian Lord hailed me in the street at Aidensfield and after our normal greetings, he posed that question.

'Is there a problem?' I asked. 'Have you got intruders?'

'Oh, it's nothing like that,' he smiled. 'But each year, as you know, we have a service where I bless the animals. People bring their pets – cats, dogs, budgies, hamsters and so forth. Well, this year I would like to extend the idea. It would be very apt if I could persuade those who use animals in their work to bring those animals to a special service. After all, the animals are being used as servants of the people and I think we should thank God for providing them.'

'Like a shepherd with his sheep? And cowman and his cow?' I said.

'Yes, exactly. I would like at least one representative of the various professions who make use of animals in the course of their work – a police dog-handler and a police dog, for example, a donkey from the beach with its owner, a racehorse and its trainer, a greyhound and its owner, a heavy horse and a ploughman, a pet-shop owner with something from his stock, an aviary keeper with a specimen from one of his cages and I was even hoping the zoo would produce something spectacular like an elephant or a zebra.'

'It's certainly a novel idea and it would add a new dimension to the service for animals.' I felt he had a point but wondered if he expected a bee-keeper to bring a bee, a snake-charmer to bring a snake, a poultry farmer to bring a hen, a fisherman to bring a fish or a rat-catcher to bring a rat. And it would be interesting to see what vets and butchers brought along, and then there were fox-hunters and rabbit-catchers to consider.

'I need to find new methods of filling the church, ways of getting bums on pews,' he said. 'We're always in need of funds too and I am sure that every time we filled the church with people attending a special service, we'd get a useful income from the collection. But my motives are not entirely mercenary – I want to make the people more aware of the varied means that God has provided for us to earn our living, and I want people to thank Him for that. And I want them to appreciate the animals which support us in our endeavours.'

'You could always hold a service for tradesmen,' I heard myself say. 'And you could have a blessing of tools – a carpenter and his chisel, a painter and his brush, a policeman and his truncheon, a builder with a brick, a surgeon and his scalpel....'

'Actually, that isn't a bad idea! A road sweeper with his brush, a blacksmith with his anvil and a washerwoman with her poss stick.' He began to enthuse over that proposal so I had to bring his mind back to the issue of the day.

'I'll have words with my friends in the dog section' I promised him. 'And I'm sure we can persuade one of them to come to church with a well-behaved animal. We do have police horses as well, you know.'

'Well, if a horse and rider came as well, it would be a bonus.' He was getting very enthusiastic about his idea.

'But if I do get a good response, I will have to find somewhere to position all the animals – we couldn't get them all into the church.'

'You'd need some drinking water for those outside, I would think. And they do make a mess, you know, if you're thinking of allowing them inside.' I had to remind him that big beasts made big messes. He'd probably need someone on hand with a shovel or two. 'And you'd have to segregate dogs from cats, and cats from budgies and I'm not sure where you'd put the elephant if the zoo produced one, or a lion....'

'Oh, I know there will be problems to sort out in advance, and indeed on the day. But the idea is not new, Nick. In the past, people used to take their animals to church with them, you know,' he said. 'It was a regular event, not restricted to special days.'

'Yes, I know, and there was a minor official called a dog-whipper. His job was to move among the congregation with a whip to keep the unruly dogs under control – and perhaps some of their owners,' I smiled. 'And there were dogs known as turnspits too; they were taken to the church, rather in the way you are suggesting for modern working animals.'

'Turnspits?' he grinned. 'What on earth were they?'

'Working dogs,' I told him. 'They were small ones, like terriers, and their job was to operate a treadmill which turned the spit which was cooking the roast over the log fire. Real hard-working little dogs, they were. They did most of the work without getting any of the benefits!'

'It sounds like a form of slavery to me,' he said. 'Anyway, Nick, you think the idea is a good one, in principle?'

'Yes, I do, and I will help in any way I can. Have you a date in mind? That would help if I am to book the police dog in advance.'

'I was intending to hold it as a summer event, we could hold it out of doors, in the church grounds if the weather was suitable. I am thinking of the last Sunday in July. I'd like to persuade our two village cricket teams to play afterwards and I'm hoping to recruit other organizations to mount displays or erect stalls. If it's a success, it could become a regular part of the church calendar. I shall refer to it as The Peacock Service.'

'Peacock?' I puzzled over the name. 'I can't see any connection between peacocks and the professions?'

'Thomas Love Peacock, the poet,' he informed me. 'In his *Headlong Hall* he wrote, "All animals were created solely and exclusively for the use of man". I can't say I agree entirely with his sentiments, but his words have provided me with a focus for my suggested service.'

'The Peacock Service. I'll remember that,' I smiled. 'Fine, so now I'll see if I can reserve that date with the dog section.'

When I rang Inspector Mason, the officer in charge of the dog section, he said. 'I've got just the dog for him, Nick. Satan. A big black Alsatian. He needs a bit of spiritual training; he's a bully, Nick, he needs to be taught Christian principles.'

'We don't want unruly creatures at the church!' I had to remind him.

'He's not unruly, in fact he's very obedient. But he's the sort of dog who, if the zoo turns up with a lion, will try to chase it off the premises. He eats cats, the bigger the better....'

'Don't you think something a bit more gentle would be a better idea?' I had to say.

'I'm joking, Nick. Satan's quite controllable really. It's more a question of availability. Two of our handlers are giving a demonstration to a security firm that same Sunday and for that we need our most experienced dogs. In addition, we have to have a team standing by for any operational requirements that might arise in the county. That leaves Satan – he's our newest acquisition, a real humdinger of a dog, built like a Shetland pony. He can sort out a whole busload of bolshie Leeds supporters by himself. He once cornered an entire coachload in the gents in Thirsk market place.'

'I can't envisage the congregation of Aidensfield Parish Church behaving like a busload of football hooligans but I am sure Satan will be an asset. So, yes, sir, I'd like to book him – I'll confirm the time in due course.'

'Consider it done, Nick. I don't think Satan's ever been to church before – and neither has his handler for that matter, so I'll get the pair of them to swot up a few suitable prayers. "Our handler, who art in Heaven ... give us this day our daily doggibix"....'

'*Deo gratias*,' I said and rang off.

During the course of the next few weeks, the Reverend Lord managed to persuade most of his intended participants to come to his Peacock Service and the advance notice in the village had generated a lot of promises. The service was scheduled for three o'clock on the afternoon of the last Sunday in July and it seemed the church and/or its ground would be full of animals who were of use to humans in the course of their work. I confirmed with Inspector Mason that Satan and his handler, PC Roger Hardy, would be attending.

We could not have the police horses that day – it was a Sunday in summer when the horses patrolled the seafront at Scarborough to impress on some of the more loutish visitors that good behaviour was a wise thing. Bad behaviour meant they could be locked up. In recent months, louts had been gathering in gangs and their unruly behaviour on the beach and in the town had upset many of the tourists. So the horses patrolled to keep these lunatics in order.

Christian Lord had succeeded in attracting some other horses, however. One was a retired racehorse called Tantalus who had a string of wins to his name and the others were a pair of giant black Shires called Black Maria and Black Prince. Their owner still used them to haul a plough and to operate haymaking equipment such as a double-horse mower. Among the other promised creatures, he had a shepherd and a sheep, a cow, calf and dairyman, a sow, piglets and pigman, a donkey and its owner, some poultry in a pen and the child who cared for them, a budgie and a pit pony that had both served down a coalmine until their recent retirement, and a retired miner to care for them, a cat which was the official mouser in a department store along with its trainer, a retired guide

dog for the blind, a performing seal from a circus which
would be in the area at the time with its trainer and an
elephant from the local zoo, plus attendant. I began to
think that an ordinary domestic animal like a dog, even if
it was a police dog, might look a shade ordinary in such
interesting company, but told myself that that was not the
purpose of the exercise. A police dog was just as important
to society as any other of the animals which would be on
display.

To accommodate his menagerie, Christian Lord
explained that he had fenced off a section of the
churchyard so that the area containing the graves was safe
from their browsing and heavy or hooved feet, and he had
organized a zinc trough which would be filled with water
for the day. As he was intending to hold an outdoor
service, a dais had been erected beside the church and he
intended to conduct the service from there. So far as
car-parking and other arrangements for coping with the
crowd was concerned, I could see no real problems.
Clearly, there would be horse boxes, dog vans,
Landrovers, trailers, an elephant truck and other
specialized transport, but after depositing their precious
loads, such vehicles could be directed to a suitable
car-park in the village for the duration of the service.
There was plenty of room.

As the day of the Peacock approached, the church and
its immediate environs took on the appearance of an
agricultural showground. George Ward, the landlord of
the pub, had erected a small marquee in an adjoining field
from where he would dispense liquid refreshments after
the event, the profits going to church funds, the WI had
organized a cake stall to raise money for the church, the
school had arranged a display of children's art in the
porch, the village first and second cricket teams were to
play against each other in an overs-match immediately
afterwards, the losing side paying to church funds £1 for
every run they scored, and other village organizations had
devised their own fund-raising schemes.

As I was emerging from the churchyard on the Saturday
before Peacock day, I encountered Claude Jeremiah

Greengrass. He was ambling past with his dog, Alfred on a long lead, and glared at me as I emerged from the lychgate.

'You're not supporting that snobby-nosed lot, are you?' he grumbled.

'What's got into you, Claude?' He was clearly upset about something.

'They say it's for professionals with professional animals. Not household pets. I asked one of the church wardens and he gave me a right look, as if to say Alfred wasn't allowed.'

'There is another service for pets; Alfred will be more than welcome to attend that one,' I advised him. 'The vicar thought it would be nice to recognize the part played by God's creatures in the daily work of the human race, so that's what tomorrow's service is about. It's for working animals, not pets.'

I felt like adding that poaching was not really a suitable profession and that Alfred's reputation, as the faithful servant of Aidensfield's most notorious poacher, was hardly a recommendation to be invited to the Peacock Service. 'There'll be police dogs there,' I said. 'And working horses, an elephant from the zoo.'

'I'm not too fond of police dogs, nor elephants,' he said. 'Not after that accident on the moor when one kicked my truck off the road.'

'They're all working animals,' I said. 'Animals that have contributed in some way to the work of the human race....'

'Like Alfred, you mean?'

'Give over, Claude! You can't say that Alfred is a professional dog in the same way that a police dog is, or a pit pony or a racehorse earning its keep or ...'

'He is, he's a guard dog,' beamed Claude.

'Guard dog?' This was a newly designated Alfred, I was sure. 'What's he guard?'

'Me for a start,' said Claude. 'And my premises, and belongings and livestock and wealth....'

'Look, so far as I am concerned, Claude, you can take your guard dog to the Peacock Service. It's nothing to do with me; I don't decide who comes and who doesn't.

Have a word with the vicar. I am not involved with the arrangements.'

'Aye, mebbe not, but you do have influence in these parts.'

Oddly enough, guard dogs were not represented at the Peacock Service although they did play an important part in our daily lives, but to describe Alfred, the lurcher and poacher's friend, as a guard dog was slightly over-doing things.

'I'll be talking to the vicar,' I promised Claude. 'I'll see what he says.'

When I saw Christian Lord, he smiled. 'Claude has not mentioned this to me,' he said. 'He must have got his rejection from one of our more determined church wardens. But so far as I am concerned, Claude can bring Alfred – he is a working dog and we must not judge our fellow creatures ... after all, dogs are not sinners.'

'Even if their owners are?' I grinned.

'Christ wants us to forgive sinners,' returned the vicar, adding with a smile, 'So far as I know, he said nothing about forgiving sinning dogs because there is no such thing as a sinning animal.'

'So all dogs, cats and other animals go to Heaven?' I put to him, as a joke.

'Don't set me off with that one!' he laughed. 'I've had enough of old ladies wanting to know if their Pekinese dog will join them in eternal bliss.'

When I got home, I rang Claude and he was jubilant. 'See you tomorrow,' he rejoiced over the phone.

'Make sure Alfred behaves himself,' was my parting retort, but Claude had already replaced the handset.

On Peacock Day, I walked along to the church to undertake some car-parking duty and was astonished at the variety of transport arrangements for an even more astonishing variety of animals. The area outside Aidensfield parish church resembled a zoo or a circus as racehorses, carthorses, hacking horses, ponies, donkeys, goats whose milk was made into cheese, guide dogs, sheep dogs, police dogs, cats used for showing and breeding, blackfaced sheep, a Hereford bull, a pair of

Friesian cows, two Highland cattle, the elephant from the zoo, pigs, assorted hens, turkeys and geese and even a snake-charmer's snake arrived. A professional magician brought a white rabbit, an animal hospital produced a hedgehog, an otter and a seal while an aquarium owner brought a tank containing a pet lobster which he'd had for twenty-seven years.

Fortunately, the churchwardens had foreseen the problems and had advised the owners to bring suitable leashes, cages or containers and the animals were spaced around the churchyard so that any innate antagonism would be minimalized. Nonetheless, there was a good deal of noise from them, varying from the neighing of horses to the trumpeting of the elephant. The arrangements were very well organized and I had no trouble directing the assorted vehicles to suitable car-parks. Last to arrive was Claude Jeremiah Greengrass with Alfred who had clearly been shampooed for the occasion and looked as if he had hated every minute of his beauty treatment. But he trotted behind his master as the service was about to begin.

Satisfied that all the guests had arrived, I left my parking duties and went into the churchyard to listen. The weather had remained kind – it was a warm and slightly breezy afternoon in late July with a few small clouds in the sky, but no sign of rain and so the service was to be conducted out of doors. The vicar came out of the church in his flowing vestments, noticed me and said, 'Thanks Nick, everything's going to plan. I've seen the collection plate already … I know we shall generate lots of income today … a good day for all, eh?'

'Yes, I'm pleased for you.' As he walked across to his dais, the organ began to play 'All Things Bright and Beautiful, All Creatures Great and Small' and all sang, including Alfred the dog, who began to howl with his muzzle pointing towards the heavens like a flue valve. The cows lowed, the horses whinnied, the dogs barked or howled, the sheep bleated, the hens cackled, the pigs grunted and the seal honked as the amplified music filled the air.

It was after the sermon, based on Job 35.11 (Who teacheth us more than the beasts of the earth?) that I became aware of a minor disturbance among the animals. It was a very small disturbance, more of flutter among them, but I worried that it might develop into something greater. Some of the animals were growing restless and becoming noisy and then I saw the cause. It was a bat, a pipistrelle. It was flittering among the outdoor congregation, alarmed no doubt by the concentration of animals and people in the place it probably used to seek its insect prey, and it had panicked. It seemed unable to find a means of leaving the airspace above the gathering of beasts and its presence was definitely unsettling some of the animals.

I think the noise generated by the crowd had probably flushed it from its roosting place in the belfry, for bats generally emerge at dusk. But it was broad daylight and the unhappy creature was fluttering low above the heads of the congregation. People were ducking to avoid it, but the vicar ploughed on with his service, apparently unaware of the growing problem. The bat seemed unable or unwilling to steer itself away from the gathering and I began to wonder how the matter would be resolved. If its fluttering presence continued to worry the animals, a full-scale disturbance might develop and we'd then have a more serious problem to deal with. I could see that the elephant was far from happy at being buzzed by a flittermouse and the seal was beginning to honk in alarm. But how does one catch a bat? Should we attempt to shoo it away?

At the far side of the gathering I noticed members of the cricket teams, already clad in their whites and caps, with the captain of the first team towering above his pals. He was Trevor Whiting, a solicitor by profession, but a first-class fieldsman who had, in his youth, played for Yorkshire. And then the bat whizzed towards him ... and in a trice, he had reached out a long arm and caught it. I had heard of cricketers instinctively reaching out to catch low-flying swallows on cricket fields, but never a bat. Without a word, Trevor cradled the creature in one big hand, took his cap off with the other and popped the bat inside. Then he folded his cap gently and held it in the closed position, knowing the bat would relax in the warm darkness. And then, as the organ struck up with 'All Creatures of Our Lord and King', a hymn thought to have been written by the animal-loving St Francis of Assisi, I felt a nudge on my elbow.

It was Claude Jeremiah Greengrass.

'See that?' He nodded towards Trevor Whiting. 'Good catch, eh?'

'Brilliant,' I said. 'He saved the day, I reckon. The elephant's calmed down, I see.'

'But that bat's not allowed here, is it?' He was trying to annoy me. 'A wild animal, not a working creature like the rest of those here today....'

'Oh, I don't know,' I grinned. 'This service is for working animals, so surely a cricketer is allowed to bring his bat?'

And Claude groaned as the combined voices of man and beast rose to the heavens.

The vicar's innovative idea of raising money through his service for working animals had been a resounding success and his Peacock Service raised nearly £850, a very useful sum indeed. But he had another fund-raising idea. He would allow brass-rubbing to be conducted within the church.

In the 1960s, brass-rubbing reached its zenith as people found themselves with more leisure time and easier access, through the motor car, to churches with interesting contents. Some wanted to do more than just aimlessly wander around during their weekends, so brass-rubbing blossomed as one hobby which provided an added interest. The notion of brass-rubbing as a hobby for the ordinary man seems to have developed around that time although a few discerning people had been enjoying it for some time before it became so popular.

In effect, the early style of brass-rubbing was quite simple. A person located a fine brass monument to a long-dead person, usually a king, queen, bishop or knight.

The brass memorial to the murdered King Ethelbert in Hereford Cathedral is a good example of one which is – or was – constantly rubbed. The king sits with his head in his hand, having had it chopped off by Offa, King of Mercia, round 794 AD.

The graves of people of distinction were often beneath the floors of parish churches, minsters and cathedrals and were each marked by a massive brass plaque set in the aisle. The oblong brass plate, generally some eight or nine feet long by three feet or so wide, bore an etched image of the occupant of the grave, invariably in full uniform, robes or armour, or in some kind of formal dress.

The name of the deceased along with his or her date of death, and probably a suitable inscription from the Bible, were usually incorporated in the design. These brass grave-covers or sometimes brass memorials without a grave and displayed on walls, were wonderfully executed and even now many of them exist with clear markings and legible inscriptions. Inevitably, some have been worn down by centuries of passing feet or rigorous cleaning, but some have been preserved in a remarkably good condition.

The purpose of brass-rubbing is to take a copy of the design on such a commemorative plaque. It is done by laying a large piece of paper over the portion of the design which is required and then gently rubbing the paper with something like a soft wax crayon, graphite or even cobbler's wax. The design on the brass is then transferred to the paper.

Some enthusiasts were content to rub only a small portion of a large plaque – say the face or a Latin inscription – and they made use of sheets of artists' cartridge paper for this purpose. Others of a more adventurous nature took along rolls of lining paper used for walls and ceilings and spread these across the entire plaque, and then spent hours rubbing until they reproduced the entire scene.

Like a length of wallpaper, these huge rubbings could then be rolled up and carried away to be later displayed at home. On the positive side, brass-rubbing did preserve the designs on the memorials, but on the negative side, the activities of thousands of brass-rubbers began to wear away the designs and rendered some of the more delicate work illegible.

Some churches, especially those with very historic or famous brass memorials, began to curb the activities of enthusiasts either by limiting their numbers or charging them a fee to take a rubbing. And that is what the Reverend Lord decided. As part of his fund-raising activities, he would charge a fee of £1 for every brass-rubbing, large or small.

The Anglican parish church did contain several interesting brasses, some being full-length epitaphs laid in the floor while others were smaller memorials attached to the walls. Brass-rubbers had been seen in the church from time to time, so it was known that the Aidensfield brasses were of interest to those enthusiasts. A charge of £1 for every rubbing did not seem extortionate. The vicar announced his levy from the pulpit one Sunday and followed it with a note in the parish magazine, posters in church plus a collecting box built into the wall and bearing the legend 'Brass-Rubbing Fees – £1 per rubbing''. Then he settled down for the funds to flow in.

None of this was remotely connected with my police duties, although every rural constable should be aware of events within his parish, consequently I knew of the brass-rubbing scheme. It was with some surprise, therefore, that while patrolling on foot in Ashfordly, I came across a full-length brass-rubbing of a fourteenth-century knight in a second-hand shop. It was not particularly well executed, in my opinion; the images were rough and rather sloppily done. I felt almost as if the entire rubbing had been completed in haste or even by a child. For a moment, I wondered if it was the work of a schoolchild, some kind of class project perhaps. From a distance, it looked passable, but did not bear close scrutiny.

Surprisingly, it bore a price tag of £5. 10s. 6d. When I looked closer, I realized it depicted the memorial to Sir Ranulph de Aidensfield, a knight who died in 1503. I had seen this memorial on the floor of Aidensfield parish church and knew where it had come from. The rubbing was done on a length of roof-lining paper with a black wax crayon. I thought little more about that brass-rubbing until I met the vicar outside the Aidensfield Stores. We chatted about parish and village matters, as one tends to do in such circumstances, and then I said, 'How's the brass-rubbing enterprise going?'

'Very slow,' he shrugged his shoulders. 'At least the income is small and slow in arriving. I'm not sure whether anyone is visiting the church to take rubbings, though; if they are, not everyone's putting money in our collecting box, although I can report a few pounds of income from that source.'

'Have you been selling rubbings to local second-hand shops?' I asked.

'I'm not that commmercial!' he laughed. 'Why do you ask?'

'I saw a rubbing in Ashfordly.' I explained what I had seen.

'Five pounds ten and sixpence?' he was shocked. 'Who on earth would charge that?'

'The shop is asking that; they'll need to make their profit on the sale. I'd guess they'd come down a bob or two if a buyer was prepared to bargain,' I submitted. 'But whoever sold it to the shop probably got two pounds ten or even three quid for their trouble.'

'Well, it wasn't me nor, dare I say, any of the parochial church council,' the vicar was adamant. 'But if people are selling the rubbings, there's clearly a market for them. I wonder if I should put some on sale in the church?'

'You'd need someone there all day to look after things,' I said.

'Yes, and I can't arrange that; it's a practical impossibility. It's a pity, Nick, that kind of profit should be going into church funds and not the pocket of some enterprising brass-rubber.'

'Or brass-neck!' I laughed.

And even as I spoke those words, the identity of a local brass-neck came to mind. Claude Jeremiah Greengrass.

The vicar smiled.

'You're not thinking of Claude, are you?' he put to me. 'It's the sort of brass-necked cheek he would employ.'

'I must admit the standard of craftsmanship was about his level,' I said. 'But he's not committing any offence by doing that, is he? Anyone can take a brass-rubbing and sell it, or reproduce it.'

'If it is him, I suppose I could ask for a share of the proceeds, for church funds,' mused Christian Lord.

'And if I were you, I'd be prepared for a massive disappointment,' I had to warn him. 'Claude is not exactly the most generous of people.'

I assured him that during my routine patrols around the village, I would pop into the church as usual, but henceforward would be extra vigilant for indications of surreptitious brass-rubbing.

I stressed I could not stop Claude, or anyone else, from taking rubbings, nor could I enforce the £1 fee, but I would be observant merely out of personal curiosity.

In the weeks that followed, I never saw Claude anywhere near the church and neither did the vicar. But I did see two more rubbings of Sir Ranulph in Ashfordly.

'Should I tackle Claude about it?' I wondered one morning a week or so later as the vicar and I were chatting.

'No, I'd rather you didn't,' he said. 'If it is him, I think he is putting his fee into the box. That is all I have asked of anyone.'

'Claude putting money in a collecting box? You can't be serious!'

'There were two £1 notes in the box last week, Nick, and you saw two rubbings for sale. I don't know if there is a connection, but I would like to think so.'

I could not believe that Claude would be so honest, even inside a church and so, next time I was on duty in Ashfordly and saw that one of the rubbings remained unsold, I went into the shop. I could not contain my curiosity any longer.

'That brass-rubbing.' I pointed to it as it was on display in the window. 'It's very interesting.'

'It's not been stolen, has it?' The sight of my uniform immediately made the shopkeeper nervous.

'No,' I assured him. 'It's from a memorial in Aidensfield parish church,' and I explained about the knight thus depicted. 'I was curious to know who the artist is.'

'It's not a very good reproduction,' said the shopkeeper, a man in his late fifties with a bald patch and a rosy round face as he shook his head. 'But I feel sorry for her. She does those at the rate of about one a week, brings them in here and I sell them. I give her four pounds for each one, poor old thing.'

'So it's not Claude Jeremiah Greengrass?'

'Him?' laughed the little man. 'He's not capable of doing this kind of work, but they sell, Constable. If I can make a few shillings I am happy, and it means that Mrs Shepherd has food in her pantry for another day or two.'

'Mrs Shepherd?'

'Her husband died about a year ago,' he told me. 'He wasn't well off; he worked on a farm. She tries to make ends meet in all kinds of enterprising ways.'

'Such as baking cakes and pies for the shop, cleaning the church for no payment and making brass-rubbings at the same time?' I smiled.

'I would think that's very likely,' he said. And I left for home. I was in two minds whether or not I ought to inform the vicar of my discovery but, after some thought, I decided that I should. After all the church could afford to be charitable to someone who was showing charity towards it.

6

'Can the Ethiopian change his skin or the leopard his spots? Then may ye also do good that are accustomed to do evil.'

Jer. 13.23

Every year, at the end of the summer term, a small group of volunteers from the Fairfax College for Boys attended a camp in the forests near Aidensfield. These were staff and senior pupils aged about eighteen. The pupils had completed their school life, so the summer camp preceded their admission to university or served as a prelude to their careers.

Fairfax College, spread across a prime site in the valley between Aidensfield and Maddleskirk, was a Catholic private school of international renown. The summer camp was one of its more recent innovations. Its purpose, apart from being a form of relaxation after the exams, was to encourage character-building, teamwork, individual skills and personal confidence. Held under canvas, the camp continued for slightly longer than a week – Friday afternoon arrival through to departure on the morning of the Saturday a week later – but it included canoeing and swimming in the three small lakes in the forest, outdoor survival techniques, moorland and mountain rescue, trekking with maps and compasses, escape and evasion exercises, rock-climbing in the Dales, wild-life recognition with particular emphasis on plants and animals which could be utilized as food, the construction of shelters and a host of associated outdoor topics.

It was a few tough days with the boys producing their own meals, and there is little doubt that it rapidly identified leaders and followers. It highlighted strengths and weaknesses, developed skills hitherto unknown and, in some cases, produced compassion for those less able to care for themselves, especially in adverse conditions. The boys clearly enjoyed it – there was always a rush of applications for the annual camp. In recent years, some of the earlier participants had returned to act as instructors with the newest intakes and there was no doubt the week-long exercise produced a high degree of cama- raderie. The police were often involved too, with their experts helping to tutor the boys in first-aid, radio communications, underwater rescue, search techniques, moorland and mountain rescue and sundry other subjects which formed part of a rural police officer's knowledge and duties. The army and RAF, ambulance service and other support services as well as skilled individuals also found themselves being asked to contribute skill and advice.

The camps had been running for some six or seven years prior to my arrival at Aidensfield and, from a police point of view, presented no undue problems. The only occasional worry sometimes occurred at the end of each camp, on the final Friday evening, when the participants had a wild party with bottles of beer and home-made food to celebrate their return to civilization on the Saturday. But that party never intruded upon the village because it was restricted to the forest and few villagers were aware of it; furthermore, the revellers were made to clean up afterwards.

The success of these camps attracted the interest of Ruth Lord, the vicar's wife. A quietly spoken but very practical lady in her early forties, she had quickly made herself extremely popular in the village. One reason for her popularity was that she had a natural ability to span the class divisions. She could relate to a working-class woman in a council house or an inarticulate farm labourer just as easily as she could attend an upper-class soiree or a middle-class cocktail party. She treated everyone with due respect and charm; in short, everyone liked and respected her.

One morning in late February I received a telephone call from her. She wanted to discuss something of importance, but stressed that at this stage, it was highly confidential. Having no idea what this might be, I said I was happy to oblige and added I would be patrolling Aidensfield that afternoon. I could pop into the vicarage if that was convenient. She said it was ideal and we agreed to meet at 3 p.m.

'Tea, Nick?'

'Thanks.' When I arrived, she led me into the lounge and settled me in a deep armchair. Beside it stood an occasional table with biscuits upon it, and within a few minutes, she produced a tray bearing a teapot, milk jug, sugar bowl and china cups. As she busied herself with serving the tea, I made small talk about the weather and village events, and eventually she settled opposite me. A slightly tubby lady with dark brown hair and sparkling eyes, she was dressed casually in a pair of slacks and a sweater and looked totally relaxed and comfortable.

'You'll be wondering what the mystery is about?' she began as she sipped from her cup.

'I must admit I have no idea why you want to see me,' I admitted. 'It's not often I get called to a mystery at the vicarage.'

She said there was no real mystery and reminded me about the Fairfax College camps, saying that she had visited one of them last summer. She had been most impressed by the entire atmosphere, particularly the spirit of comradeship and happiness which had been generated among the boys.

'I know those boys are from upper-class homes,' she went on. 'They are public-school boys from affluent backgrounds and they are the offspring of accomplished parents, but it did occur to me that other boys might also benefit from the camps.'

'From comprehensive schools you mean?' I asked.

'No,' she said. 'I wasn't thinking so much of those children. I was thinking of those with a more deprived background. Borstal boys in fact.'

'Borstal?' I cried. 'But they're the real hard cases, Ruth. They're the ones who have appeared before the courts many times and are sent to Borstal because there's nowhere else to put them.'

'Yes, I know,' she said. 'But I am sure some of them would benefit from the kind of experience produced at the camps. There must be some benefit in mixing with educated boys of their own age, learning that there is a world other than crime and deprivation and actually experiencing that kind of world, even if it is temporarily in a tent in the middle of a forest. Some Borstal boys have never spent a night in a tent, nor have they explored the countryside. They know nothing about caring for others, nothing about working as a team....'

'I don't think the villagers would take kindly to convicted youths being allowed to roam free in the forest – and be close enough to Aidensfield to break into a few homes and shops.'

'I know there'll be opposition, Nick, which is why I wanted to test my suggestion on you before I took it any further. I don't envisage a lot of Borstal boys coming here ...'

'If too many did come, they'd take over the camp,' I warned her. 'Some of those hard kids can be extremely violent. They'd finish up running the camp for their own purposes, bullying the schoolboys into submission.'

'I can see the risks, but those selected would have to prove their worth before they came,' she said. 'I suppose the Borstal governor could select them following their good conduct over an extended period, or they might volunteer, of course. They might be the ones almost due for release but if, say, five or six came as an experiment, that might provide us with some idea whether the scheme would succeed.'

'So what do you hope the Borstal boys will gain from this experience?' I put to her.

'A broadening of their outlook, a chance to meet people from different backgrounds with different ambitions, an opportunity to spend time in the countryside learning new skills, finding their own weaknesses and strengths ... those camps can provide the ideal opportunity, Nick. They are designed to build character and to give confidence to youthful people – precisely the sort of things needed by some of those deprived kids.'

'And who would take responsibility for the Borstal boys while they are here?' I asked.

'That would be decided by the college in consultation with the respective Borstal governors. Maybe they would not need to be supervised the whole time?'

As she tried to persuade me about the merit of her ideas, I was recalling the many pieces of ancient wisdom which could be summarized in the old saying that a leopard will not change his spots. I'd known of earlier experiments of this kind, one where a council estate had been built next to some upper-class homes in the hope that the council-house occupants, who had been moved there from an inner city slum, would emulate the upper-class householders. And it had been a disaster – the upper-class neighbours had been tormented until they had left ... and a councillor had said at the time, 'If you put a dog in the same sty as pigs to teach 'em good habits, the pigs will soon make the dog as mucky and greedy as them. Experiments like that never work.'

My immediate reaction was that there was every chance that the boys of Fairfax College would learn unsavoury things from the Borstal boys during such an experiment. That was the way that life tended to operate. But it was not my decision – I was being quizzed as a kind of barometer of local feeling.

'I anticipate lots of problems, Ruth, along with some opposition from the village. You'd have to reassure the people in all the surrounding villages that the incomers would not present a threat. Borstal boys are real hard cases, you know, they're not merely approved school types.'

'But they are just boys,' she added.

'Older boys,' I corrected her. 'Young men. Men up to the age of twenty-one. Senior youths who were sent to Borstal after a life of committing serious crime and rejecting the norms of society.'

'But they're not beyond reform, Nick, not if they are placed in the right environment and given the right kind of encouragement. I think some of them deserve that chance. That is why I want to give it to them.'

'Have you spoken to the headmaster of Fairfax about it?' I asked.

'Not yet. I wanted to test ground opinion first, Nick. You, in other words, you have the ears of the village.'

'I admire your ideals, Ruth, but there are practicalities to overcome. So do you want me to go round and float the idea? I can test it upon the villagers and come back to you with their response.'

She smiled. 'No, that would kill it before we even got going. I just wanted a gut reaction for starters. I need to know what kind of opposition there will be.'

'Some of the villagers might not be too antagonistic,' I said. 'They might be willing to tolerate the Borstal boys camping nearby so long as they stay in the woods and aren't allowed to roam the village. From a police point of view, that would be my immediate reaction. Let them come, restrict them to very small numbers and have them very carefully supervised at all times.'

'You're painting a gloomy picture already, Nick,' she spoke quietly.

'You must appreciate the kind of youths we're talking about. To qualify for Borstal training, they must have committed a serious crime – not petty stuff like larceny or vandalism, but real crime – burglaries, housebreakings, crimes of violence, rape, that sort of thing. Most of them are at least seventeen years old and they're up to twenty-one – at twenty-one, they'd go to prison for the same crimes. These lads are locked up for a minimum of six months; they are the really tough cases, Ruth, the hard men of the future. Most are beyond reform; they don't want to change their way of life.'

'If it's reform we're talking about, then there's all the

more reason to give it a try. Say, Nick, that I suggested to the head that he invites six Borstal boys to join his campers this year? Under strict supervision? Would you object, from a police point of view?'

I had no idea whether she was going to use my opinions as a fulcrum when she discussed it with the headmaster, so I emphasized that I was speaking from a personal point of view. My private reservations were not the formal reaction of the police service, nor of my local force, I told her. For an official response, she would have to approach the chief constable.

I did express an opinion that I could not foresee any major problems if the Borstal boys were under constant and close supervision. Whether a hardened Borstal trainee from a deprived inner-city background would adopt a new lifestyle through being in close proximity to a privileged youth from a private school was the type of question which would provide hours of theorizing and discussion.

In practical terms, it was the actual implementation of the idea that would provide some of the answers. And no one could guess what they would be, least of all a village constable.

In the weeks that followed, Ruth Lord discussed her proposal with the headmaster of Fairfax College who in turn had discussed it with the chief constable, the chairmen of the parish councils of Aidensfield, Maddleskirk and Elsinby, and the governor of a Borstal Institution situated on the Yorkshire Wolds. The governor said he welcomed the initiative and agreed with the vicar's wife that there were some youths in his care who might benefit from associating with young people from a background which differed subsbtantially from their own. The outcome was a formal meeting at Fairfax College involving the headmaster, Ruth Lord, myself and other interested parties such as my divisional inspector, the chairmen of the neighbouring parish councils, representatives from the East Riding Borstal and several of the Fairfax College teachers who undertook the responsibility for running the Fairfax camps.

The meeting decided that six Borstal boys would be invited to the next Fairfax College summer camp. The boys would be carefully selected from those due for imminent release, this being thought a sensible reward for their continuing good behaviour prior to that release. The camp was scheduled for the middle week in August and the Borstal boys would be accompanied by two warders. The warders would be expected to participate in the activities – indeed, one of them was a champion cross-country runner and the other an expert in rowing.

Both were Home Office approved physical fitness instructors. Their input would be useful to all the campers. Rudolph Burley, the auctioneer and chairman of Aidensfield parish council did express concern about security of village properties and the safety of some of the village girls if any of the Borstal boys ventured unaccompanied into Aidensfield but assurances were given that the selected boys would not be considered dangerous to the community, and that they would be subjected to constant supervision.

After a lot of sensible discussion, the scheme won the necessary approval and Ruth Lord was delighted. Her next request was for permission to visit the camp at mutually convenient times to see whether any progress was being made. No one could see any objection to this. In fact, it was felt that the occasional presence of a mature woman would provide a calming influence to the boys and so Ruth's project became a reality.

Having entered the dates of the camp in my diary, I made a conscious decision not to visit the camp in uniform. In the eyes of the Borstal boys, that might be seen as provocative or a sign of distrust at a time when they were expected to display trustworthiness coupled with good behaviour, and so I decided to keep my distance – under normal circumstances, I would not have visited the Fairfax camp anyway unless requested for a specific purpose. When the date of the camp arrived, therefore, I wondered what the outcome would be. In my mind, it represented a strange mix of strong but youthful male humanity. I hoped it would not prove an explosive mix.

In the village there were one or two mutterings and grumblings from the local people, some of whom worried about burglaries, housebreakings and assaults upon their daughters and wives, while some of the businessmen were concerned about break-ins at the garage, the pub or the shops. I knew that if we did get a crime of any kind during that week, it would be blamed upon the Borstal boys, whether or not they were responsible. I found myself praying that no such crimes occurred – I had no wish to visit the camp to interview anyone about crimes committed in the locality. Like Ruth Lord, I wanted the Borstal boys to show the rest of us that they could be trusted, and I wanted the villagers to give them that opportunity. A lapse by just one boy could put the whole scheme in jeopardy.

During the week, I saw Ruth cycling off to the forest to monitor what was, in effect, her own scheme. She spent a lot of time at the camp, or accompanying the boys on outings such as the long hike or the rock-climbing expedition to the Dales and then I experienced the first hint of concern. It came from Gerry Burns, one of the athletics masters at Fairfax College. He was involved with the running of the camp and I met him by chance when I popped into the pub for a leisurely pint on the Thursday evening.

'How's the camp progressing?' I asked after the small talk had evaporated.

'As enjoyable as always, Nick. They're a lively lot this time, really keen to get stuck into tasks. Wonderful to work with, all of them.'

'Borstal boys included?' I put to him.

'They've fitted in very well,' he said. 'There was a bit of mutual mistrust at first – that was inevitable, with each side eyeing up the other and putting them to the test, usually verbally, but soon they found common ground and within a day, there was no distinction. The projects involving teamwork were excellent and I must say our lads responded extremely well and I think some firm friendships have been formed.'

'I'm pleased it's all worked out.' I sipped my beer. It was

beautiful, like nectar. 'I must admit I had some reservations.'

'We didn't exactly expect a troublefree time,' he agreed. 'But there weren't as many problems as I expected. But you're not having any trouble from the Borstal boys, are you?' he asked as we stood at the bar, each enjoying our pints.

'Not the slightest,' I said. 'So far, so good, touch wood!' And, jokingly, I tapped the wooden surface of the bar counter.

'The vicar's wife has taken a shine to one of them,' he grinned mischievously. 'She's never away from him. And a fine big strapping lad he is too. Handsome and intelligent, she's gone for him in a big way!'

'Helping him, you mean?' I had to ask.

'More than that, I'd say, Nick.'

'I don't believe it!' I had to defend Ruth. 'She's a middle-aged woman, the wife of a vicar, highly respectable.'

'It happens,' he said solemnly. 'Women fall for younger men, it happens all the time.'

This was something I had never expected and something I could not envisage. If Ruth Lord had so ardently desired her scheme to be a success, the last thing she would do would be to compromise the entire operation by fooling around with a lad half her age, or less. But there was no accounting for love ... I knew that too. Like all policemen, I knew that middle-aged women did sometimes fall desperately in love with younger men, often those with a reputation for daring and a disregard for authority. Such women often responded to a total change from their ordinary domestic routine. On several occasions during my police service I had had to deal with bouts of the domestic turmoil which had resulted from extra-marital relationships. But Ruth Lord?

'I'll believe that when I see it for myself!' I tried to dismiss the possibility from my mind yet I could not ignore the possibility that it might have happened. I must admit that the revelation bothered me and if Gerry had put that kind of interpretation upon Ruth's behaviour, then there might be some truth in his assertions. On the other hand, her actions could be totally innocent. Having aired this topic, we turned our conversation to other matters and eventually went home.

Although I had momentarily been concerned about Ruth's alleged behaviour I felt I knew her well enough to be certain she would not indulge in an affair with a Borstal boy, no matter how charming, persuasive and attractive he might be.

But on Friday lunchtime, while I was on duty and in uniform, I was driving past the vicarage on my way home for lunch and saw Ruth with a tall, handsome young man.

They were walking towards the church. He was wearing hiking gear and carried a rucksack on his back. I knew that Friday was the day of the big hike. The end-of-camp party would follow tonight. For the big hike, it was the practice for the lads to make an early start, around 8 a.m., therefore the group of hikers would be well into their trek and be several miles from Aidensfield by this lunchtime. So if this was a Borstal boy, had he bunked off, to use schoolchildren's jargon? Was he one of the Fairfax pupils? Or someone else? I had to find out. I had to know if Ruth was leading him astray.

I halted my police van and climbed out. Ruth saw me and stopped, then she came towards me and, after a short hesitation, so did the youth.

'Nick,' she beamed, and I could see the excitement in her eyes and in her demeanour. 'So nice to see you.'

'Hello, Ruth.' I looked at the big youth and he did not meet my gaze. He would be at least twenty-one, I guessed, a senior inmate who was serving the final weeks of his sentence. 'I saw you and thought I'd ask how the camp was progressing.'

'Wonderful,' she beamed. 'Absolutely wonderful, it's been a huge success so far … oh, and this is Wayne Buckle, he's attending the camp.'

'Hello, Wayne.' I held out my hand for him to shake and he hesitated, not looking me in the eye, and then Ruth said, 'Go on, Wayne, Mr Rhea won't bite!'

The big youth took my hand and shook it with a

powerful grip; he was about six feet three inches tall with shoulders like an ox and hands like shovels.

He had close-cropped dark hair, blue eyes and ruggedly handsome features which would cause any woman to day-dream about him. His appearance was the kind that might have been found in a male model or a film star, but I could not imagine this giant of a man fulfilling either of those roles. He looked more like a lumberjack to me.

'Enjoying the camp?' I asked him.

'It's great,' he said and now he looked at me. 'It really is, Mr Rhea. The best thing that's ever happened to me.'

He had a strong Liverpool accent, I noticed and was clearly nervous of my uniformed presence. Clearly, he was not one of the public school boys.

'I'm delighted, but it's all down to Mrs Lord. It was her idea.'

'I know, it's brilliant.'

'So what do you do back home?'

'Nothing. Hang about the streets, get into bother.'

'And now? After being on this camp?'

'Look for work, a career. Better myself; I can, I know I can now.'

'I hope you do, Wayne. I wish you all the best. So you're not going on the big hike today?'

'No, I got excused. Ruth, Mrs Lord, is showing me her library and things in the church, so I can think about a career.'

'Wayne is very keen on road building, Nick.' When she mentioned this, I saw him blush as if she was betraying one of his secrets, but she continued, 'I felt his interest was sufficient to get permission for him to not go on the hike today; his mentors gave him permission to spend the day with me, looking at books! Now, you see, when Wayne was very little, he was brought to our moors by a friendly neighbour and saw the Roman road in Wheeldale. That fascinated him, and he's often thought he'd like to build a road but, well, the opportunity has never presented itself. So today, I am showing Wayne how to research the subject of roads – my husband has several books in his library, including one about the history of the Great North

Road, and in the church, there is a map on the wall which shows the green tracks of the moors, as they were in the sixteenth century. I want Wayne to be able to do his own reading when he gets back to Liverpool; they have a very good library service in the city, and want to give him an inkling on how to discover things for himself.'

'I'd never been in a library,' he said. 'I never thought about how roads came to be here.'

'I've got some books as well,' I said. 'Some about the law of highways and others on their history. If you've time to pop in sometimes, I'll show you them.'

'But you're a copper!'

'So?'

'Well, coppers don't help people, do they? I mean, I'm in Borstal and here's you saying you'll let me into your house and look at your books....'

'Yes, that's exactly what I'm saying, Wayne. If I can help you to make yourself a career building roads, then I'll be delighted to do so.'

He just stood and blinked; it was as if I was giving him a million pounds and I wondered if anyone had ever offered to help him before, rather than to tell him what to do or what not to do.

'Can we pop around after lunch, Nick?' Ruth took the initiative.

'Sure, I'll be in.'

I was now positive that Ruth Lord had no romantic designs on this big youth and was equally sure that this youth would respond to her assistance. When they came to my house, I took Wayne and Ruth into the lounge, never referring to his past before my wife and children, and showed him my modest library of books. I had some about toll roads, others showing the history of roads in the north of England, several about the Great North Road, its history and lore, along with stories from the coaching days, one about lost roads, another with the history of road building.

Wayne sat on the settee surrounded by my books and I said, 'Wayne, what you need now is a list of these. Then, when you go home, you can ask for them at the library.'

'Ruth's got some of these, Mr Rhea.'

'You can learn a lot from books,' I said, providing him with a pen and some paper. 'Make a list of these and then you've got something to start with when you go home.'

They stayed about an hour and Mary made them a cup of tea, and then they left, with Ruth saying she was driving Wayne into Ashfordly to have a look at the library there.

'Thanks, Mr Rhea.' Wayne shook my hand again, this time with more strength and more friendliness. 'When I get out, can I come and see you?'

'Yes, do that. And let me know how you are getting along, keep in touch.'

When they had gone, I found myself thinking that Ruth's scheme had worked, if only for this one youth. He seemed so enthralled with books and with road building that I knew she had set a deprived lad firmly on a new style of life. I wondered if a week had been long enough for him to re-think his future, but perhaps it had. Perhaps a week away from Borstal, away from his companions and away from the infuences of his past life had been sufficient for him? In the very brief time I was with Wayne, I had found him likeable and sincere – although I did wonder what he had done in order to be incarcerated in a Borstal Institution. I could have found out, by checking with CRO, but decided that would be intrusive.

The following Sunday, I saw Ruth Lord walking someone's dog through Aidensfield and hailed her.

'This is Bonny, Mrs Popplewell's retriever. Mrs P's ill – a bad dose of flu, so I volunteered to walk her dog, didn't I, Bonny?' She smiled as I approached her. The dog wagged its tail at the mention of its name.

'Wayne returned to Borstal, has he?' I asked.

'Sadly, yes. Thanks for showing the human side of policemen, Nick,' she said. 'He'd never been in a policeman's private house before, and you made a hit with him. But he is a perfect example of a youth going wrong because he's been reared in the wrong environment. He's known nothing else but criminality since his childhood – his peer group at home are all petty criminals or worse –

but in just a few days with the Fairfax boys, he realized that his future lay in his own hands, not in state institutions and officials. Once he's released from Borstal, he's going to look for work – you know they're building lots more motorways in this country? Well, Wayne wants to work on those.'

After he'd gone back to Borstal, I heard nothing more from Wayne although Ruth did receive the occasional letter; the first came within a week of him leaving the Fairfax Camp and was a thank-you letter, he even asked that I be thanked for my part in his new realization. Then there were long gaps until one letter announced his release from Borstal and said he was now back in Liverpool with a firm intention to begin his career. Then Ruth heard nothing more. I know she was disappointed because she'd felt sure her protégé would maintain contact and even seek advice, but there was an ominous silence. I do know she wrote to the address he'd given on his first letter, but got no reply. Then, about eight months after Wayne's return to Liverpool, she received a telephone call from the governor of the East Riding Borstal. It was to say that he'd been informed by the authorities in Liverpool that Wayne was back in police custody having been arrested in a stolen car after a raid on a building society in Huyton.

I must admit I was disappointed too. Of all the criminals I had met, I had believed that Wayne would have the sense and determination to abandon his old way of life in favour of something more worthwhile; the lad had seemed so genuine, but it seemed that both Ruth and I had been wrong. For me, the disappointment was not as great as that felt by Ruth Lord – for her, apart from any personal disappointment, Wayne's lapse could be used as evidence that the joint Borstal/Fairfax camps were not a viable option.

I was not told of the precise circumstances of his latest lapse into crime and neither was Ruth, but we knew it could result in Wayne being returned to Borstal for a further period of so-called training but, if he was more than twenty-one years old at the time of his latest offence, he could be sent to prison. There was no word from Wayne, either by telephone or by letter and I do know that Ruth was profoundly hurt by his apparent lack of consideration for her.

Perhaps he had no idea she had been told of his lapse? Perhaps he had taken advantage of her kindness while in this area, only to reject her once he was back on his own familiar patch of England?

And then, one morning in early March the year following Wayne's camp, she got a telephone call. It was from Wayne Buckle and it was from a telephone kiosk.

'Can I come and see you?' was all he said after introducing himself.

'Yes,' was all she was able to reply before his money ran out which meant she had no idea when he was coming, or how, or whether he wanted to stay in the village.

She rang me, clearly experiencing some uncertainty about the wisdom of accommodating this wayward youth, but all I could say was, 'It's obvious he wants you to help him. Let's see what he wants.'

Wayne Buckle arrived during an afternoon two days later having hitch-hiked from Liverpool and he went straight to the vicarage. I have no idea of the conversation which followed but within a couple of hours, Ruth rang me and asked if I could pop around for a chat with her and Wayne. I went as requested and found him sitting on the settee, unkempt and dirty after his journey. He rose to his feet as I entered – I was in uniform, but he extended his hand and I shook it.

'Hello, Wayne,' I said, without making any reference to the information I had been given about his escapade at home.

'Mr Rhea,' he settled back on the settee. 'It's good to be here, believe me.'

'Wayne has something to tell us, Nick,' Ruth said and I could see that the gloom of the past few weeks and months had evaporated. She was back to her usual cheerful self.

It seemed that, upon his release from Borstal, he had returned to Liverpool, to live in a small flat he was renting, but very quickly had found himself back with his former colleagues and mates. At first, it had been fun, doing the rounds of the pubs and clubs, conning bits of cash from people, stealing more when funds were low and then had come the escapade in the stolen car.

Wayne said, 'I tried to stop them, Mr Rhea. It was then I realized I was returning to my old ways – with my mates all around there was no way I could avoid it. They put pressure on, you know how they do that. They nicked a car and picked me up, for a ride they said – I had no idea it was nicked, by the way, not at first, and then they went for the bank raid. Clubs and pick-axe-handle job it was. I wanted no part of it; I asked to be let out but they said no, I was to go along with them. So I did, I had no choice; they raided a bank and got away with cash, lots of it, but the police was waiting. We all got nicked. With the loot. I got three months in prison, Mr Rhea. I'm not complaining, I deserved it. I shouldn't have let myself get back into the old ways … but that job stopped me in my tracks and I remembered Aidensfeld and Ruth and the camps and things. So I decided the only way to keep my nose clean was to get away from my mates, from Liverpool, start a new life.'

Ruth said, 'Christian and I have said Wayne can stay here, at the vicarage, until he gets somewhere of his own. He wants to look for work, Nick, and that's why I asked you to call in. You know people at County Hall, don't you?'

'Yes, several.'

'How about the Highways Department? Any contacts there?'

'There's an old schoolfriend of mine, I'm not sure of his official status there, but he does work in the Highways Department. Wilson is the name. Jim Wilson.'

'Can I ask you to contact him, to see if there are any vacancies now or in the future?

'They've been advertising for staff a lot in recent months,' I said. 'A lot of the county's roads are being upgraded.'

I rang my old schoolmate, Jim, and explained the

situation, giving a full account of Wayne's history and his
latest brave decision. The outcome was that the Highways
Deaprtment of the County Council was currently advertising for staff and there were vacancies in all kinds of
disciplines for skilled and unskilled workers. I was told that
if Wayne cared to send for an application form, it would list
the range of openings and he would be given every
consideration, irrespective of his criminal record. Within a
month, Wayne had secured a job on the maintenance
section of the County Highways Department and he was
delighted; he found himself a rented cottage in the countryside near Bedale and went off to begin his new life. He did,
however, return to the Fairfax Camps to help with some of
the work and to advise some of the newest Borstal inmates.

During this time, he did keep in touch. Eventually, he
bought a small car which he cherished because it was his
very own and soon found himself promoted. Wayne
Buckle was the happiest man alive, I felt; it wasn't long
before he was courting one of the secretaries from the
department and within two years, they were married. I was
best man.

Two children followed, then Wayne Buckle applied for a
more senior post with a motorway construction company –
and was successful – but kept moving to better positions.
As I compile these notes in 1996, he is aged 54 and is
chairman of a thriving motorway construction group of
companies.

In spite of a very busy life which takes him to every area
of Great Britain and overseas, he does keep in touch.

But Wayne Buckle took advantage of the opportunities
that were presented to him and although he gave thanks to
Ruth Lord for her vision of a better life for lads like himself,
much of his success was due to his own efforts and a
realization that the only way for him to succeed, was to
abandon his former life of crime by moving to a new
district.

And even now, whenever he goes for a walk upon the
North York Moors he always visits the stretch of highway
that gave him inspiration years earlier, the old Roman road
at Wheeldale near Goathland.

7

'He that hath no sword, let him sell his garment and buy one.'

Luke 22.36

During the 1960s, there was a renewal of interest in the past coupled with particular emphasis upon the so-called simple life. Young people were attracted to the notion that it was judicious to abandon a life of material things, consequently they began to flout the conventional rules of society and live in communes. Some stuck flowers in their long, unwashed hair and called themselves flower people – one Yorkshireman actually thought the flowers grew in their hair – 'Wiv all that muck about, yon flowers'll be well fertilized,' he remarked.

Those members of the new society embraced a culture of peace and free love, which in reality meant fighting the police on CND rallies, taking drugs, challenging authority and having sexual relations with almost anyone or anything. Others opted out of what might be described normal society to live a life in the open air and on the open road, leaving their litter and junk behind for tidy-minded and more realistic people to clear away.

At the same time, there was a corresponding move towards nature, even by the most conventional of people. This resulted in townies rushing into the countryside to buy tumbledown cottages with a bit of land so they could be self-sufficient in beans, potatoes and pigs. Fortunately, the true country folk, who were very realistic and wise, retained their old, infinitely more practical ways and made useful sums of money from these deluded aesthetes before they packed up and returned to town.

It is difficult to determine whether society gained any benefit from the abandonment of self-discipline during the 1960s – perhaps we are only now beginning to suffer from that – but what did happen was that lots of forgotten customs were remembered and revived. Many had been discontinued during the World Wars and there developed a feeling that quaint memorials of the past should be restored as a symbol of happier times.

One of them was the Aidensfield Sword Dance. A village incomer called Aubrey Fletcher, who ran a flower shop in Ashfordly, had purchased an old book about the North York Moors and in it had found a reference to the sword dance. It was only a fleeting reference but it did say that the Aidensfield Sword Dance was held on the village green at noon on Plough Monday. Sadly, the book, published in 1834, did not provide any further information although the nature of the reference did suggest the dance was being held at that time, i.e. 1834.

Within rural Yorkshire, similar dances were still being practised earlier this century, some of the participants displaying their skills in popular competitions. In the 1960s, the Goathland Plough Stots were one surviving example – and continue to this day. Possibly the oldest surviving team of its kind in Britain, its origins date from Viking times more than 1,000 years ago, when long-sword dancing was associated with a fertility rite. It was thought that the clashing of swords drove away evil spirits. The word 'stot' means bullock and this name was given to young men who, in modern times, tow a plough around the village on Plough Monday as they sing and dance to raise money for the church and local charities.

Today's Plough Stots number about thirty young men and they are an amalgamation of the earlier stots and a local sword-dancing team; they continue to give lively displays in North Yorkshire's Esk Valley and have visited venues in other parts of Britain and the continent, always raising money for local charities. There used to be a sword dance in Ampleforth too and, in the 1960s, an attempt was made by a monk to revive this one, with little success.

Other sword dances, morris dances and mummers' plays were held across Yorkshire, some as open-air dramas and others merely as dances, consequently the Aidensfield Sword Dance was not unique in its time. There are strong links between Plough Monday events, mummers' dances, sword dances and morris dancing, the chief ones being that they devolve from a ritual associated with fertility of crops at the death of the old year and the birth of the new. In Christian times, Plough Monday, the first Monday after the Epiphany which is on January 6, marked the beginning of the farming year. It was the day when farm labourers returned to work after the Christmas break. Ploughs were blessed in church and there were other associated events.

But, like so many ancient customs, the Aidensfield Sword Dance had ceased long ago and all modern records had been lost. Aubrey Fletcher, a small, thin and bespectacled man in his mid-fifties who bred Yorkshire Terriers, decided to do something about it. His first approach was to visit the older residents of Aidensfield to ask if they remembered the dance or had any recollection of their forebears talking about it. Surprisingly, none did.

His efforts were rewarded with little more than shaking heads and forthright statements that they knew 'nowt about that awd dance'. He even approached Aidensfield's oldest resident, ninety-seven-year-old Mrs Maud Crabtree. Born in 1868, she had a remarkable memory for events in and around the village, having lived there for the whole of her long life, but when Aubrey mentioned the sword dance, she shook her head and similed. 'I know nowt about it and neither does anybody else, so there's no point in asking, is there?'

It was during a visit to his flower shop in Ashfordly during March, when I wished to buy a bouquet for my wife's birthday, that he told me of his fruitless endeavours. As I listened to Aubrey, I began to wonder

why the village's own sword dance had been so
completely eliminated from the folk memory of the
community. Usually in this kind of circumstance,
somebody in the community would have been expected to
possess a relic of such an historic custom – in this case, I
would have expected somebody at Aidensfield to have
had cuttings from old newspapers, one or two of the
swords, some remnants of the costumes used, souvenirs
of family links, that sort of thing. But, according to
Aubrey, no one knew anything nor had they kept any
relics; worse still, no one appeared willing to even talk
about the sword dance. All his enquiries had produced
absolutely nothing. I must admit I thought this was very
unusual.

I did begin to wonder if there ever had been an
Aidensfield Sword Dance. Could the author of the book in
which Aubrey had found his reference have made a
mistake?

There was a village in the West Riding of Yorkshire
called Austerfield but I had no idea whether that village
had ever sported a sword dance and besides, Austerfield
and Aidensfield did not sound very similar – although
some author's bad handwriting might have led to
confusion about their names. That was a remote
possibility, a very remote one.

'Mr Rhea,' said Aubrey as I had a coffee with him that
morning. 'You get out and about a lot in the course of your
duty. Can I ask you to keep your eyes and ears open for
any reference to the sword dance? You get into people's
homes; you'd think somebody would have a keepsake of
some kind. Maybe you could ask on your rounds? You
know,' he added confidentially, 'I almost got the
impression that people did not want to talk about it – the
older people, I mean.'

'Covering something up, is that what you're saying?' I
asked. 'Why would anyone want to hide the fact that a
custom as harmless and historic as a sword dance had
taken place in their village?'

'My sentiments exactly, Mr Rhea,' he spoke with a note
of triumph. 'I am now wondering whether I have

uncovered some ancient secret about the sword dance, and it makes me more determined to get to the truth of the matter.'

'I can't imagine that kind of secrecy being a valid reason, Mr Fletcher,' I said. 'Things like old customs – sword dances or any other sort – usually fade away because nobody bothers to maintain them. In our case, two world wars have intervened, with our young men – the dancers – being called up for service in the armed forces and perhaps being killed, so there's little wonder the sword dance has faded away.'

'But if that was the case, surely the villagers would have wanted to revive the dance as a memorial to their fallen heroes?' he suggested.

'That's a point,' I conceded. 'So all we're left with is a brief note in an old book which tells us the dance was being practised in 1834, more than a hundred and thirty years ago?'

'That's it, nothing else,' he admitted. 'Not even the remotest of links remains in our village, and I find that very odd indeed.'

I knew that lots of practices and customs had died away over the centuries, many being casualties of wars, and I was sure that lots of other villages had once boasted a range of events which were no longer held. I did wonder whether Aubrey was reading more into this than was the real case – perhaps the Aidensfield Sword Dance had faded away simply because no one was interested in it. That could have happened a century ago, in which case few memories would linger. I remained a while to chatter with him and then a lady came into his shop seeking an indoor plant for a friend, and so I made my exit. But I did promise Aubrey that I would remain alert for any references to the sword dance or any associated memorabilia that I could find.

Then about six months later, two odd things happened. As is the case on so many occasions, the events themselves seemed unrelated but the long arm of coincidence can be very strange. The first was a chat with the vicar, The Reverend Christian Lord.

'I am thinking of having a service for Blessing the Plough on Plough Monday, starting next year,' he said during a conversation about village matters. We had regular chats of this kind, one of which was to identify people in need of help; my job took me into lots of houses where I could identify the needy and in such cases, I always made sure the relevant authority was informed, often discreetly. Sometimes that meant a quiet word with the vicar or Catholic priest.

'The official start of the new farming year?' I said. 'I'm sure it will be a success. You might get a few farmers into church!'

'Most of them around here are Catholics,' he said. 'The farmers, I mean. The Reformation missed them on their lonely farms on the moors. They've kept the old faith down the generations and, as you know, the farms are passed down from father to eldest son. So there are very few Anglican farmers hereabouts.'

'So you're having doubts about the value of such a service?' I put to him.

'Well, there's never been a Plough Monday service for as long as anyone can remember. I've been going through the old records in my library and can't see any reference to a Plough Monday service this century. I'm sure there must have been one at some stage.'

'Did you check back further?' I asked.

'No, I ran out of time. Why? Do you think there's value in going back further?'

I told him about the mysterious Aidensfield Sword Dance, last known to have taken place in 1834, and added, 'If there was a sword dance, which has associations with Plough Monday, you'd think there would be a Plough Monday service to bless the ploughs.'

'Absolutely right, Nick. I'll keep looking, but whatever I find or do not find, I think I will hold a Plough Monday service next year. It will remind others, who are not farmers, that we owe such a lot to God's gift of the landscape around us. So all I shall need is a plough to bless, preferably without a tractor attached! One of those old horse-drawn ploughs would be perfect.'

'I'll see if any of the farmers on my patch have a spare one!' I joked.

But it was that joke which produced the second coincidence.

During Novermber I was visiting all the farms on my patch to check the stock registers which had to be maintained by all livestock farmers. At that time of year, many of the farmers were busy ploughing the fields of stubble which were the legacy of their corn harvests and so the fields comprised rich dark-brown furrows in a series of remarkably artistic designs. The countryside was being transformed from yellow, tan and dull green fields into a patchwork of rich glistening browns which, by the following spring, would produce bright new green shoots. For the mechanized farmers of the 1960s, much of the ploughing was completed long before the traditional Plough Monday. I wondered how that would affect the vicar's proposed Plough Monday service.

It was during this busy time for farmers that I called at Peat Rigg Farm, Aidensfield, the loftily situated holding of Harry and Winifred Bosworth and their son, Gerry.

Their farmhouse and buildings nestled in a sheltered hollow in the moors and the entire complex was hidden from the passing roads, but the Bosworth spread of fields and open moorland covered an elevated and huge area, some of which had once been used for peat cutting, hence the farm's name. The Bosworths, always busy, kept Highland cattle, blackfaced sheep, Tamworth pigs and masses of poultry, in addition to their arable farming. I always liked to visit Peat Rigg because Harry invariably invited me to share a walk around the complex, after the traditional cup of coffee or tea with masses of fruit cake, scones and cheese – a snack by their standards. The contents of outbuildings of farms as large as this one were endlessly fascinating and in some ways reminded me of my childhood explorations of my grandfather's farm.

On this occasion, Harry did not fail me. 'Howway, Nick, let's have a paddle around,' he said.

It was a chilly November day and I could see his son, Gerry, guiding his tractor across a field to the north of the farm. He was turning over the earth with smooth, confident movements, the heavy plough coping easily with the tough moorland soil. We were heading for one of the outbuildings where Harry was in the process of cleaning and maintaining some of his harvesting machinery. I marvelled at the cleanliness of the farmyard and its immediate surrounds. He really did set an example to others. Inside the massive stone structure, there were some dismantled pieces of mysterious agricultural equipment and he told me he was cleaning the bits, then greasing them for storage until they were required next year.

'There isn't an old horse-drawn plough among that lot, is there?' I indicated the pieces which were strewn across the floor.

'Aye, as a matter of fact I have one next door. It's in that middle shed,' he said. 'It's horse drawn, it's not been used for tens o' years. My father kept it in mint condition, though, greased and cleaned and painted up where necessary. I've never used it. Here, come and have a look. Anyroad, why are you interested in awd ploughs?'

I told him of the vicar's plans to revive the Plough Monday tradition and he said, 'Well, we're not Church of England as you know; our family was living in these parts long before them protestants came along, but t'parish church can use this plough if t'vicar wants. I've no objection to that. I can't see t'point of blessing it, mind, when it doesn't do any work these days. He'd be far better off blessing a milking machine or a tractor or a combine.' And he chuckled at his own logic.

Inside yet another spacious, dry building full of sacks of cow nuts and smelling delicious, he indicated a point midway up the rear wall. There was a kind of stone shelf which had been formed where the thickness of the stone of the sturdy base wall gave way to a thinner one above. And there was a beautiful old plough, its bare metal parts gleaming and its red paintwork looked brand new. A double furrow plough, it had two slippers, otherwise known as mouldboards, each with a gleaming metal sock; there was a pair of long twin wooden handles, painted red, with a coulter and a red furrow wheel, red land wheel and red beam.

It was fully equipped with a three-horse baulk, complete with cutwillies and highly polished cobbletrees and swingletrees in natural wood. They were chained to a large hook in one of the beams above but it meant the plough was well off the floor and safe from any risk of damage.

'It's like an exhibiiton plough; it doesn't look as though it's ever been used!' I went nearer to examine this gem. 'It's the sort of thing you'd find in a museum.'

'Nay, I don't think it's ever been worked,' he said. 'We never used it, but my dad said we had to clean it and keep it in good condition.'

'But why keep it in such beautiful condition?' I asked.

'We're its custodians, it's t'awd sword dance plough,' he said.

I felt a termor of excitement now. 'What old sword dance?' I asked.

'Our sword dance! Aidensfield Sword Dance,' he said. 'It's never been done for years, but that awd plough was t'centre-piece. They allus danced on Plough Monday and did a frantic sort of dance waving swords about and dancing between 'em on t'ground, while yon plough stood in t'background. Summat to do with fertility rites, they reckon, from Viking times. Pagan really, not at all Catholic.'

'So why have you got this plough?' was my next question.

'When they stopped t'sword dances, all t'gear they used was distributed to t'surviving members of t'group,' he said. 'Some got a sword apiece, we got yon plough. One of my ancestors was t'leader, you see.'

'When was that, Harry?' I asked.

'Nay, long before my time,' he said. 'I couldn't rightly say when it was but I think it was my grandfather who was given yon plough, so I reckon it was before t'turn of t'century.'

'So why did the sword dance come to an end?' I put to him.

'Nay, that's summat I never did find out, Nick. I remember my grandad would never talk about it, nor would anybody else. They just stopped doing t'dance years back, but I've never asked why. And my awd dad's dead and buried now, and I don't think he ever knew either. If he did, he never said.'

'Have you anything else connected with the sword dance?' I asked. 'Papers, lists of dancers, the routine they used, the music?'

'Nothing, Nick. Just that awd plough. I've nowt to prove where it came from, neither, except word of mouth, but I don't think any of my folks would lie about a thing like that.'

'So the swords might still be in the village as well?'

'It's very possible, but I wouldn't know where to start looking,' he said. 'You'll have to find t'descendants of them that did the last dance. Eight dancers, there was, my dad said, so there should be eight swords somewhere. Anyway, why all t'sudden interest in t'sword dance and Plough Monday?'

I told him about the vicar's intentions and mentioned Aubrey Fletcher's desire to revive the Aidensfield Sword Dance but I could see this did not please him.

'He's an incomer, eh? Trying to show us locals how to live our lives, Nick. Well, if he wants my advice, he'll drop them plans. Tell him to leave well alone.'

'You do know something about the sword dance!' Now, I realized he knew more than he was prepared to admit even to me – for I was an outsider too.

'Just tell Mr Fletcher he's best leaving things as they are,' said Harry. 'Mebbe you would see him and tell him, from us all, friendly like.'

'If I knew why there is likely to be such opposition to the revival of something as simple as an ancient sword dance, it would make all this much easier to understand,' I put to him.

But Harry merely shook his head. 'It's best left alone, take my word, Nick. Just tell him to leave things as they are, let sleeping dogs lie. Isn't that what they say?'

'I'll pass the message on,' I promised him, and prepared

to leave the farm.

There is no doubt that Harry's attitude increased my curiosity about the sword dance and I found myself sharing Aubrey's interest in discovering the cause of its lapse. In the weeks that followed, I maintained my interest and continued to ask around the village, but it became increasingly clear that the elder residents of Aidensfield, along with those whose famiies had lived here for generations, were most anxious that memories of the dance should not be stirred. I became acutely aware that any revival of the sword dance would never be welcomed. But I had no idea why.

My police duties prevented me from conducting any prolonged sessions of detective work into the mystery of the sword dance, although I popped into Aubrey's shop from time to time to update him on my discoveries. The old plough at Peat Rigg was of great interest to him – but we never found any of the swords.

He had found one other reference to the dance; it was in a *Handbook for Rail and Road Travellers*, a guidebook to the area published in 1894, but the wording was such that it did not say whether or not the dance was then being held. The relevent paragraph said, 'Part of Aidensfield's long history is rooted in the ancient sword dance held on Plough Monday. Dating from Viking times, the dance may have had bygone associations with pagan fertility rites'. That's all the book said about it, leaving it somewhat uncertain as to whether the dance was being held at the time the book was written. From the wording, it was unclear whether the word 'held' was in the present or past tense.

As Christmas turned into New Year, and the vicar went ahead with his Plough Monday service, I did consider researching the dance in back copies of the *Ashfordly Gazette*. The snag with the cessation of such a dance was that it was unlikely to attract the interest of the newspapers of the period. The fact that the dance was not held during a particular year would not appeal to a newspaper published a few miles away in the nearest market town and in any case, to wade through weekly newspapers seeking such snippets of local information going back a century or so would be enormously time consuming. I began to think I would never discover the reason for the puzzling end of the Aidensfield Sword Dance and concluded that the secret, if there was one, lay within one or more of the houses which comprised the village of Aidensfield.

It was Alf Ventress, Ashfordly's longest serving constable, who unwittingly gave me the next clue.

He was settling down to his lunch in the office, giving himself a break from some clerical chores, which meant I could use the typewriter. Because it was year end, each country constable had to submit an annual return of the crimes which had occurred on his beat. This listed them in order of the Home Office classification and noted which, if any, had been detected. In my case, there were few crimes that year – no murders, rapes, burglaries, robberies or arson had been committed on my beat, although I had had one or two instances of simple larceny, a couple of garage-breakings, one housebreaking and two cases of actual bodily harm. All had been detected, for which I was thankful.

It was during my typing-up of the statistics sheet in Ashfordly Police Station, that Alf Ventress said, 'It's been a quiet year on Aidensfield patch, Nick, judging by your return.'

'Perhaps a bit quieter than average,' I said, watching Alf crack two hard-boiled eggs by crashing one against the other. 'But that's a sign of efficient policing....'

'The snag with that theory,' laughed Ventress, 'is that you do your job so well that there are no crimes – you prevent them happening – which means the bosses look at the crime figures for your beat and decide that because there is no crime, a constable is not required! You can work yourself clean out of a job if you're not careful, Nick.'

'And if there is no resident constable, there is no one for the locals to report their crimes to. That's another way of keeping the figures low – you just don't let the crimes be reported!'

'The trick is not to be too clever with figures, Nick.

Aidensfield could do with a serious crime or two if the presence of a constable is to be maintained there. That's how the village got its first constable, you know. Because of a serious crime. The Murder That Never Was, that's how the newspapers described it. The chief constable of the time, and the lord of the manor, thought that Aidensfield was going to become a den of iniquity, so they installed a constable there. And it's been quiet ever since.'

'A tribute to a succession of efficient constables,' I grinned. 'So what was the Murder That Never Was?'

'A fatal stabbing, Nick, with a sword of all things. In Aidensfield! It happened during a festival of some kind – I noticed it in some old files I was clearing out a few months back. Murder files.'

He was now tucking into his two hard-boiled eggs, dropping bits of wobbly egg-white all over his uniform to lodge among the ash of umpteen cigarettes.

'A sword you say?' My mind immediately thought of sword dancing.

'Yes, it was during a sword dance, if my memory serves me right. They used real swords in those days, long swords with points and sharp blades, not those blunt things they use now. I remembered that case because of its association with the Aidensfield constable. One youth stabbed another to death. Big stuff in Aidensfield.'

'So have we still got the file?' I was excited now.

'It'll be in the loft somewhere, the space above the cell passage. There's cardboard boxes of them, dozens of old files going back to when the Force was founded in 1856. I've written "Murders" on a few boxes; it's in one of those, 1900 or thereabouts. I can't remember the exact date but it's easy enough to find.'

It didn't take long to get the keys to the police station loft. As Alf Ventress had said, the boxes of Murder files were easy to locate even in the restricted light of a solitary bulb, and it was simply a case of searching through them until I came to the one marked 'Aidensfield, 1901. Murder. R v Barnes'. I took it down to the office where I could study it in more conducive surroundings and untied the string around the heavy brown folder.

Immediately inside was a newspaper cutting, yellow with age but with the print still legible. The headline was 'Aidensfield Farm-Worker Acquitted' with a secondary headline of 'no evidence offered on a charge of manslaughter'.

Couched in the quaint language of the time, the cutting told the story of twenty-five-years-old Edwin Barnes, a farm-worker who lived with his wife and his parents at Blue Wath Farm, Aidensfield. A member of the Aidensfield Sword Dancing team, he had been engaged in a hectic dance routine on Plough Monday during which a nineteen-year-old labourer called Joseph Lumsden had been killed with a blow from a sword. The point of the weapon had entered his stomach regions to cause a massive wound resulting in severe bleeding. He had died from loss of blood before reaching hospital. Lumsden was the nephew of Mr and Mrs P. Willis of Frost Hollow, Aidensfield, a farm in a deep valley to the east of the village.

Lumsden had been working for his aunt and uncle at the time, and he lived at their farm. He was also a member of the sword dance team.

Upon the evidence gathered by the police, the crown prosecuted Barnes for murdering Lumsden, the chief evidence and motive being that the deceased had been secretly visiting Barnes' wife, Juliet. Juliet was pregnant at the time of the incident, the allegation being that the child was Lumsden's. It was said that Barnes used the cover of the sword dance to murder Lumsden, doing so in the guise of a tragic accident.

Murder was then a capital offence, but following Barnes' own version of events, it seemed that there had been a tragic accident with Barnes losing his footing during a fast-moving sequence and stumbling with his sword outstretched. The point had entered Lumsden's stomach to cause massive wounds of his internal organs. Other members of the dance team, and several spectators had been called to give evidence but Barnes' defence councel had, during cross examination, persuaded the jury that Lumsden's death was a tragic accident. There was no proof that the unborn child belonged to Lumsden, and no proof of an affair between him and Barnes' wife. The jury was asked to discount the rumours of an affair and after due deliberation, found Barnes not guilty of murder. As there was no alternative charge of man-slaughter, he was acquitted in spite of the inquest verdict of 'murder by person or persons unknown'. It was a highly controversial verdict and it divided the village, some believing Barnes to be innocent and others firmly of the belief he had murdered Lumsden in cold blood under the cover of an accident while sword dancing.

It was the aftermath of this case which had brought the Aidensfield Sword Dance to a premature end. Its continuation would remind the village every year of the tragic events of that Plough Monday and so it had been decided to bring the custom to a conclusion. Because of the powerful local feelings, the families and personalities involved, the village has never talked about it since that time.

In the file, I found another note from a constable which said that after the verdict, Barnes and his wife moved away from the area to work on a farm in Northumberland and nothing more was recorded of them. His mother and father, however, continued to live at Blue Wath Farm and during my time at Aidensfield, the farm was still owned and farmed by members of the Barnes family.

So far as Frost Hollow was concerned, the family was no longer called Willis or Lumsden, so I did not know whether the present occupiers had any connections with that old case. Even so, there was every possibility that relations and descendants of both families continued to live and work in or near Aidensfield.

Having made my discovery, it was easy to anticipate the local distress which would be created if Aubrey Fletcher managed to revive the Aidensfield Sword Dance. For my part in the affair, I felt it necessary to inform him of my findings. I replaced the files in the police station attic and told Alf Ventress of my discovery. He agreed with my intended course of action and said he would not mention the case to anyone else.

Aubrey was in full agreement.

Now that he understood the reluctance of the villagers to talk to him, coupled with the roots of the problem, he decided not to pursue the idea of a sword dance revival. I did inform the vicar of my findings too, because it had some bearing on his Plough Monday services; he decided to go ahead with his ceremony of Blessing the Plough, but understood the reason for not referring to the long-abandoned sword dance.

And there the matter rests.

The Aidensfield Sword Dance has never been resurrected, but to this day no one knows for certain whether young Joseph Lumsden was murdered or whether he died in a tragic accident. Quite simply, no one ever talks about it.

8

'This is the generation of them that seek him.'

Psalms 24.6

There has long been a belief in urban areas as well as rural, that memorable incidents tend to come along in threes, rather like city-centre buses. Nothing happens for ages, then it all happens at once, usually with three examples of a particular event occurring in rapid succession. A variant of this is that bad things happen in threes or that one severe disappointment is followed by two others. Even one's domestic appliances tend to break down in threes – if the cooker develops a fault, you can guarantee the kettle and washing machine will expire very soon afterwards.

The superstition about bad things coming in threes is said to have arisen after St Peter denied Christ three times but that apart, country people will say that if a death occurs within their village, it will be followed very quickly by a further two. Likewise if a traffic accident occurs nearby, then it will be followed by a further two. Having worked as a policeman, I know it is remarkable how many times this old belief comes true, with nasty things frequently happening three times in rapid succession. Time and time again, I have dealt with a sudden and unexpected death, only to have to cope with a further two in a very short time. Some years ago, there was a succession of RAF plane crashes within the county; they always seemed to occur in threes. Three crashes in as many weeks was one example, and then several months passed without another and then came a further three within days.

It is certainly very odd.

It was with this kind of thing in mind that I pondered the odds that such a sequence could happen following the story of the sword dance death in Chapter 7. In that case there was the problem of keeping secret an event which had happened in the past. For the finest of motives, secrecy was maintained in the belief that the circumstances of the killing be kept from modern descendents of the families involved. Contemporary sensitivities would be protected.

But suppose a highly embarrassing event had occurred in the midst of a family of, say, only a generation or two ago? Should the present generation be told about it? And if so, by whom? If the indiscretion had come to the notice of the police, should the police inform a bona fide enquirer about the known facts, or should they keep such secrets for ever? I found myself pondering the morality of this on two similar occasions which arose very soon after the revelations of the Aidensfield Sword Dance death.

The first concerned a family who were trying to trace their ancestors, or to be more precise, it was the wife of the couple who was conducting the search for her forebears. The couple were Martin and Kathleen Melrose and they came from Staffordshire, Kathleen's maiden name being Barr. Although born and reared in a village not far from Stone in Staffordshire, Kathleen had once heard her Grandmother Barr say that her ancestors hailed from villages within the North York Moors. During her childhood, Kathleen Melrose had heard her granny mention the names of several villages in and around the moors, one of which was Aidensfield.

Kathleen's juvenile attempts to persuade Granny to provide further details had failed. She wouldn't say anything else about that part of her life. Determined to solve the mystery of her links with the North York Moors,

Kathleen had therefore established the practice of visiting the moors villages during weekends and even during her holidays. She was fortunate in her mission because her husband provided his support, along with the necessary finance and transport.

In the 1960s, the hobby of tracing one's family roots was very much in its infancy with little professional assistance available to such researchers. Thereafter, genealogy developed to such an extent that, by the mid-1990s as I compile these notes, it has developed into a thriving activity supported by magazines, professional advisers, computer-aided research facilities and clubs with thousands of enthusiasts.

But in the 1960s when Kathleen Melrose was trying to find her roots, the hobby usually meant long hours of diligent research in old churchyards, musty parish records and local newspaper files, particularly the notices of births, marriages and deaths. There was all manner of official records to trace and peruse after gaining official access. Not forgetting Somerset House which was the office of the Registrar General and central registry of the nation's birth, marriage and death certificates. There was the thrill of asking ancient people to trawl their memories for the tiniest of snippets of information and the greater thrill of discovering someone who could remember something of importance and then securing that link with some kind of supportive documentary evidence.

The whole affair is rather like a perpetual criminal investigation, with a complete family tree being the distant and sometimes impossible objective. Some researchers persist in their quest because they feel their ancestors have connections with the royal family or the gentry of the region, others wanted to know if their family has produced someone famous, adventurous or in other ways meritorious, and others just want to know about their hazy origins.

But most, if not all, must begin their quests in the knowledge they might uncover something most unpleasant about their forebears; many, I am sure wonder if they will rattle an infamous skeleton in the family cupboard.

And that was the problem with the researches of Kathleen Melrose née Barr.

As a village policeman, I was rarely involved with the people who came to search Aidensfield parish records or who came to scour the tombstones for names and dates. That kind of thing was the vicar's problem and responsibility but Martin and Kathleen Melrose were more determined than other compilers of family trees. For them – or for Kathleen to be precise – it was almost an obsession and my first contact with them came one wet Friday morning in March. Someone rang the bell of my office door and when I responded I found a dripping couple standing there. Each would be around forty, I estimated, the woman being more generously built than the man. He was a thin fellow with a tiny moustache and rounded spectacles; she looked the picture of health and happiness with a ready smile and blonde hair peeping from beneath her hood.

They were dressed in waterproof hiking gear complete with coats, leggings and boots, and around the man's neck was a map in a plastic folder. I thought they were hikers seeking a recommendation for a bed-and-breakfast establishment or perhaps coming to report a lost wallet or some other item of personal property.

'Come in,' I invited them.

'We're dripping wet,' said the woman. 'And our boots are dirty – we won't come in, thanks, we've only a small bit of information for you. It'll only take a minute.'

'Oh.' I wondered if they had witnessed something I should know about. 'So how can I help?'

'We are Mr and Mrs Melrose,' the woman told me. 'From Staffordshire, and we are staying at Elsinby, in the Beckside Guest House. For the weekend.'

'Yes?' Lots of people stayed in local guest houses for the weekend.

'We are seeking my wife's ancestors,' said Mr Melrose. 'We shall be searching the churchyards at Aidensfield and Elsinby and maybe some others if we have time, and we might be knocking on the doors of some of the residents to ask if they can remember members of the Barr or Sinclair family – Barr was Kathleen's grandfather's name and her grandmother was a Sinclair. And if we can find a starting date or two, or a name, we might ask the vicar if we can see the parish records.'

'I see,' I said.

'We like to tell the local constable what we are doing,' continued Mr Melrose. 'In case he gets reports of suspicious activities in the churchyards or churches. We look at memorials in the churches too. Some of the local people might be suspicious of us, wandering around graveyards or spending along time in village churches, or peering at village houses and chatting to people.'

'Oh, I see. Well, thanks. I'm pleased you have taken the trouble to inform me.' It was a thoughtful gesture. 'I do hope you find what you are looking for.'

'Have you been here long?' was his next question.

'No,' I said. 'I'm not a native of Aidensfield, so I have very little knowledge of the family histories of the local people, although I do know that a lot of them are related. But if I can help, then of course I will.'

Having informed me of their presence during the coming weekend, they went off and I saw them trudging in the rain towards the churchyard. To notify me of activities which might be construed as suspicious was most thoughtful and I hoped their search would produce something useful. I made a quick note in my offiical diary, highlighting their address at Elsinby should I wish to contact them for any reason, and then went about my own daily routine. After dealing with the morning post and a few circulars, I prepared for a day's duty, my patrol that morning coincidentally being around Aidensfield and Elsinby. In such a compact area, I'd probably encounter the couple during my rounds.

I did.

Within a couple of hours, I was plodding through the rain in Elsinby, heading for an address where I had to interview a lady who had witnessed a traffic accident in York, when I saw the Melroses. They were leaving the churchyard as I approached and although I was some distance away, I hailed them.

'Any luck?' I called.

'A little, there's a lot of Barrs in this churchyard but no Sinclairs, at least not in the period I'm checking,' shouted Mrs Melrose. 'We've got a note of the tombstones and we've some more to check before we get our heads stuck in parish records.'

'You don't start with parish records?' I asked.

'No, we try to shorten our investigations by getting a firm starting date if at all possible, that's where tombstones are so useful. And they often give us the full names, ages and dates of death of the deceased. Some give the year of birth too, or the means of calculating it. That's the best way of getting a good start. There's a good chance that most of the graves we've found are distant cousins or relations of mine,' she told me.

As we were having our chat, a muddy Landrover halted at my side. It was Jim Ross, a farmer from High Barns at Elsinby. Ruddy-faced, flat-capped and in his late fifties, he wound down his window and asked, 'Are you heading my way, Nick?'

'I'm in the village for a while, I can call if you want to see me.'

'Aye, there is summat I'd like to talk to you about. I'll be home in ten minutes or so, I'll make sure Jenny has t'coffee on!'

And he drove away as I took my leave of the Melrose couple. Within half an hour, I was sitting in the spacious kitchen at High Barns enjoying one of Jenny Ross's scones and a big mug of milky coffee. As we chatted, it emerged that Jim's nephew, who worked on the farm at weekends, was thinking of joining the police service and he wanted some information about the police service as a career. He was anxious to know the qualifications required, the salary offered, the promotion prospects, how to make application and the distinctions between the various police forces throughout Britain. I was happy to explain things to Jim who would pass the details to his nephew, and I promised I would get our recruiting department to send some literature to the lad in due course. The nephew, called Philip, wasn't there as we had this chat – he'd taken some calves to Northallerton Mart.

As I was saying my farewells in the yard outside, Jim followed me to my minivan and said, 'I saw you chatting to that couple near the church. Quizzing you, were they?'

'Not really.' I then wondered if Jim's ploy to get me to his farm for a chat was really because he wanted to discuss the Melrose couple! 'They're researching their family tree. They came to see me this morning, just to let me know they're in the area for the weekend, and what they are up to. I was asking about their progress.'

'Barrs. She's looking for Barrs.' He adopted a serious expression.

'And Sinclairs,' I added.

'You know about them?' he asked.

'Sinclair was her grandmother's maiden name, she married a Barr. The lady I was talking to is Mrs Melrose from Staffordshire, that's her husband with her. She was told by her grandmother that her family originated in this area,' I informed him.

'You'd tell her nowt, I would think?'

'I don't know anything about her family,' I said. 'I couldn't help them.'

'Aye, well, they've been here, to my house, asking, but I said nowt.'

'Why have they been here?' I asked him.

'This farm used to be in her family,' he said. 'A hundred years ago that was. Sinclairs. She'd found that out but wanted dates and names. But I said I knew nowt about it. I bought the place off a chap called Sanderson whose family got it from the Sinclairs way back, but I never told her that. I just said I knew nowt about things back beyond Sanderson.'

'Why aren't you willing to tell her what you know? Why pretend you know nothing, Jim? She'll find out one day; there's all kinds of records she can locate. The information's all there, all she has to do is find it. It'll take her some time, but she's the sort who'll never give up.'

'Mebbe so, but it's best they don't get it from us, Nick.'

'Best they don't get what?' I asked.

'You don't know, then?'

'I know nothing, but what is it that it's best I don't know.'

'Well, if you don't know, you can't tell 'em, so I shan't tell you then you can't tell them. I reckon that's the best way of dealing with it.'

'Jim, you've lost me now! What are you trying to say?'

'I'm trying to say that some folks is best knowing nowt, and if you know nowt, you can't let the cat out of the bag, can you? So I shan't say owt to you, then you'll never let things slip.'

'You're trying to tell me there's a family secret – her family secret – and it's connected with this farm? Is that it?'

'I'm saying nowt,' he grinned.

'And I'll say nowt either,' I assured him.

'Things is best left as they are,' he nodded sagely. 'Sleeping dogs and all that.'

'I suppose you are right,' I said after this odd interchange.

The snag with discovering there were unsolved mysteries in the district was that anyone, especially a police officer, would then want to find out what had happened. I was no exception. I could not really think of anything that was so bad it should be concealed from members of the family concerned, especially when it was in the past and they were making legitimate enquiries into their own background. Whatever the family secret, had anyone – especially someone who was not related – the right to hide such information from the descendants?

As I continued my patrol of Elsinby village, I pondered the mystery which had come to my notice and wondered how I could discover what it was.

If the local residents refused to talk to descendants of the family concerned, it was hardly likely they would confide in a policeman, particularly one who was not born and bred in the district. This was not the first time that a village has collectively decided not to reveal things to outsiders – police officers on murder enquiries have encountered it from time to time. But this was not a murder investigation and although it was no concern of mine, I began to wonder if a piece of subterfuge was called for. When I met the postman, Gilbert Kingston, later that morning, therefore, I tried to elicit some information from him.

'Morning Gilbert,' I greeted him. 'Nice day.'

'Not bad for the time of year,' he said, as he often did. We chatted for a few moments about nothing in particular, and then I said, 'Gilbert, there's a couple wandering around the village, a Mr and Mrs Melrose from Staffordshire. Tracing their lost relatives.'

'I've seen them,' he said. 'We've had a chat, not that I could help.'

'Did they ask about High Barns?'

'What do you know about High Barns, Nick?' Quite unexpectedly, he adopted a very defensive attitude.

'Nothing,' I had to admit. 'But I've just come from there and that couple had been to see Jim, about their ancestors.'

'Well, I hope he told 'em nowt....'

'He told them nowt and he told me nowt,' I said. 'So it all makes me wonder what there is to hide.'

'Some things are best left alone, Nick, and I should have thought a policeman would know that. Now I don't know whether these Staffordshire folk will ever find out what they've come to unearth, but if they do, they won't get it from any of the folks hereabouts, not those who have lived here all their lives anyroad. Take that from me.'

There was a distinct air of coolness and finality about his attitude and I got a similar response from George Ward, landlord of the local pub. Sam Cook the cobbler, Harold Poulter the undertaker and Doctor Archie McGee. They were all local men of many years standing but none would say anything about the mysterious events at High Barns long ago. It made me even more determined to find out what had happened but I knew it was something I would never be able to discover in the short course of a single weekend. It would require several weeks of fairly diligent and secretive enquiries. For one thing, I had no desire to upset or antagonize the villagers.

I knew, of course, that all the sources of information which were available to the Melrose couple were also available to me and I was sure that, given time, they would eventually exhaust all their avenues of investigation – and they would discover the secret which was currently being kept from them. If so, it was pointless me following in their footsteps – but I had additional sources of information, i.e. police records. I became determined to uncover the High Barns secret, if only for my own satisfaction.

The North Riding of Yorkshire Constabulary had been founded in 1856, a little more than a century earlier and most police stations had kept written records of every occurrence with which its officers had dealt since that time. Some large leather-bound books, full of data in beautiful copper-plate handwriting and dating from that era were still on the shelves of many rural police offices. One was a list of executions – dating from 1856, it listed offenders who had been dealt with at committal proceedings before Ashfordly Magistrates Court and who had later been executed after a trial at York Assizes – and those who had been executed had the word 'hanged' in red ink beside their name.

Another equally ancient book was a handwritten list of every inn and public house in the petty sessional division, with details of the type of licence held and the landlord's name. Another was a list of local villains and ne'er-do-wells, also dating to 1856, some of the surnames being familiar even today. There was a lot of social and criminal history on the shelves of Ashfordly Police Station – and lots more stored in brown paper parcels in the attic above the cells.

The problem was that I had no idea what I was seeking. I asked Alf Ventress, whose knowledge of local police matters was encyclopaedic, whether he was aware of any incident, long ago, which was associated with High Barns at Elsinby, or with people named Barr or Sinclair. He shook his gnarled old head.

'Sorry, Nick, I've a pretty good knowledge of local affairs and folks, but not those from Victorian times or earlier. Sorry.'

I knew that whenever Sergeant Blaketon was out of the way, and I was on duty at Ashfordly Police Station, I would have to plough through those old records, not knowing where or when to start or what to look for. But that's how discoveries are often made. So that is what I did.

During the months which followed, I systematically searched every old book on the police station shelves without finding any reference to the name of either Barr or Sinclair and then set about a similar search of our ancient files. The volume of work in the early days of the Force was far less than in modern times and so the files were fewer. Fortunately, they were listed upon a simple index. Under the Crime main heading there were lots of sub-titles including Murder, Arson, Malicious Damage, Robbery, Burglary, Rape, Sacrilege, Housebreaking, False Pretences and so forth. There were subject files such as Inquests, Brothels, Carriers' Licences, Explosives, Fugitive Offenders, Hackney Carriages, Pound Breach, Street Lighting, Road Accidents, Mantraps, Weights and Measures, Magistrates' Courts, Public Nuisances, Missing Persons, Intoxicating Liquor, Knackers, Children and Young Persons, Aliens, Animals Wild, Domestic and Diseases of, Obscene Publications and many, many more.

More mundane files included maintainance of the police station, decorations to police houses and similar subjects. Quite clearly, I could ignore a high proportion of these; furthermore, Kathleen Melrose was about forty, I reckoned, which suggested she was born in the mid-1920s. That would suggest her parents' era was around the turn of the century, probably earlier.

Thus if she was seeking information about a period beyond her own parents', i.e. her grandparents' and great-grandparents', it would be prior to 1900 – and as the Force records went back only to 1856, this considerably reduced my area of search. The files had been tied together in bundles – for example, all the Murder files were stored together and dated from 1856, with a file for each year until 1956. Those from 1956 until the present time were kept in the current system. Thinking that the worst possible thing that could happen to a family was the crime of murder, I started with those files. It took a long time, but I found nothing associated with either High Barns, the Barrs or the Sinclairs. Likewise, rape, arson, burglary ... I found nothing. In the weeks which followed, whenever I was on night duty in Ashfordly or had time to spare from my routine duties, I plodded meticulously through the files, but found nothing that would provide a lead. In the meantime, Mr and Mrs Melrose continued to visit the area in their quest, although I rarely saw them. My local network of informants acquainted me with their visits.

In the case of some of the files at Ashfordly Police Station, papers were missing, probably having been removed to be added to more recent case-files with which they were linked. But the officers of the time had not endorsed the files with the location of the removed items, so it would not be easy to trace the missing papers, if indeed they had been retained. I began to think I was trying to achieve the impossible – and besides, I kept reminding myself, it was really nothing to do with me.

'Do you know what's the most common crime?' said Alf Ventress one Sunday morning as we were working beside one another in the office at Ashfordly. Sergeant Blaketon was enjoying a weekend off and I knew he'd gone to Blackpool for a break. I was surrounded by a pile of old files, having now reached 'Coinage Offences', and he was grinning at my endeavours.

'Stealing,' I said. 'Larceny, simple larceny to give it its official name.'

'Wrong,' he said with a smile. 'Try again.'

'Assault? Common assault?'

'No, it's incest, Nick.'

'Incest? But you rarely see a case of incest in court, Alf!'

'Exactly. That's because it's kept quiet, Nick. It's kept within the family, in a manner of speaking. But criminologists and welfare workers of all kinds, 'specially those concerned with cruelty to children and associated problems, will tell you that incest – especially involving children – is the most prevalent of any crime. Kids with unexplained bruising and injuries, young girls running away from home, lads running away as well, going off to London for the bright lights, lads being awkward or turning to crime ... there's a whole host of juvenile troubles which are caused through incest, but the victims never talk, Nick. They've been frightened or tricked into silence, so we are never told. The true instance never comes to light. Families ensure it's kept under wraps.'

'Are you saying I should be looking into that?'

'Speaking as a very experienced police officer and a man who has spent his lifetime in this part of the world, I would suggest it is worthy of your consideration, Nick. And that is precisely the sort of thing a family would want kept secret, isn't it?'

'Do we have a file on cases of incest in this area?'

'If we have, it'll be in that loft among the others.'

I went straight up to find it and there were folders dating to the origins of the Force, but they contained very few papers. Like the files I had examined previously, there were papers missing and I assumed they had been removed to be added to more recent case papers. Nonetheless, I searched the records from 1856 until 1900, but there was no record of either the Barrs or the Sinclairs beign involved in an incest investigation. It was a good try, but it produced nothing. I thanked Alf and continued with my steady search of the other files.

It would be six or eight months later by the time I reached the files headed 'Missing Persons' and there, to my delight and astonishment, I found a reference to Thomas Sinclair of High Barns, Elsinby. It was dated 1863 and it seemed that Thomas, then aged thirty-three, had simply walked out of the house and vanished. My heart began to beat – the period was right. I felt I had begun to solve the mystery. I had a name, an address and a date, always a good start to any enquiry.

The first papers in the file was a missing person form which had been completed by the police inspector then in charge of Ashfordly section. His name was Inspector Bernard Horner.

The date of the form was Wednesday 4 March, 1863 and

it comprised a series of boxes which had been filled in by the Inspector. The person making the report was named as Hester Sinclair, 30 years of age, of High Barns, Elsinby. The missing person was Thomas Sinclair, 33 years of age of the same address, described as a farmer. Following the sequence of the form, I learned he had last been seen at the farm on Sunday 1 March 1863 around 7 p.m., having completed the milking for that day. Hester had been upstairs tending her baby at the time and Thomas had not even said goodbye.

There followed a physical description of Thomas – stocky build, dark-brown hair, a healthy complexion, dark-brown eyes, good teeth, moustache and sideburns, wearing brown corduroy trousers, dark-brown boots, a white shirt with long sleeves and no collar, a dark-green waistcoat and dark-brown jacket. Neither his horse nor any of his personal belongings were missing, his nightwear was in his bedroom and no firearms were absent from the house. That suggested he had not intended to harm himself, and indeed, there had been no such indication in his behaviour. The hat he sometimes wore was hanging on a peg in the hall, another indication that he had intended to return.

His absence was therefore odd, and it had taken Hester a few days to contact the police because she thought he would return – he would often go for long walks alone in the surrounding countryside which he knew intimately, and she thought he had done so on this occasion. Initially, she had not been concerned when he had not returned and she had gone to bed at 9 p.m., falling to sleep immediately as she'd had a tiring day with her child, but when Thomas had not returned for milking the following morning, she did begin to wonder where he was; a further worry was that he had not taken anything with him that might be used during an extended absence. It was at that stage she wondered if he had come to some harm.

In the file, there was a note to say that the police had checked his usual visiting places – the blacksmith's shop, the inn, neighbouring farms, the village store and all likely places, but he had not been seen at any of them following his departure from the house. The stationmaster said Thomas had definitely not taken a train anywhere and several people in Elsinby, and on the surrounding farms along the routes he usually walked, had been interviewed by the police, with no sightings of Thomas being reported. A thorough search of the farm and its entire range of buildings had been undertaken without success, and there had also been a physical search of the countryside around Elsinby. That had been done by the police and teams of villagers who were familiar with the landscape and all places of risk, but Thomas had not been found.

The report added that there was no reason to think that Thomas had harmed himself, the general belief being that he had been involved in an accident after leaving home for one of his long walks. The odd thing was that no one had reported finding him in an injured condition, and none of the hospitals or doctors in the vicinity had treated him. In the file there were several continuation sheets, each saying that further enquiries had been made, but it became clear to me that Thomas Sinclair had never been found, dead or alive.

Local enquiries had continued for six months after his disappearance with more leisurely enquiries continuing for a further nine months or so. But of Thomas Sinclair, nothing had ever been found. Even so, that particular file had never been closed.

I made a copy of the salient details and returned the file to its place. I felt quite proud that I had discovered Thomas Sinclair, even though the mystery of his disappearance had apparently not been solved.

A few days later I had to visit the vicarage at Aidensfield. During my conversation with the vicar, I recalled the visits by the Melrose couple and asked The Reverend Lord, 'You remember Mr and Mrs Melrose? From Staffordshire? They came looking for their ancestors?'

'I remember them well, Nick. Nice people, but very persistent. They've been back several times.'

I told him about my discovery and he said, 'Well, that explains part of the mystery,' he smiled. 'The Melroses knew about a Thomas in the family and felt sure he would be buried either here or at Elsinby, but I administer both churches and have searched our records – there's no sign of his grave in any of the local churchyards, neither is his death registered with us. Having heard your story, I now know why!'

'And their baby? Was it baptized at Elsinby?'

'Yes, there is a Maud Sinclair in our registers; she was baptized in 1863. I found that entry for the Melrose couple. That child was the grandmother of Mrs Melrose; it was she who told Kathleen Melrose about the local family connections.'

'So they have examined all your registers?'

'Thoroughly; they found records of Maud's birth and christening, but no birth or christening for either of her parents – clearly, they came here from another parish. I could not find any record of the marriage of Thomas and Hester, probably for the same reason, although after Thomas disappeared, Hester remarried. Thomas was declared dead after nothing had been heard of him for seven years. He does not have a grave in any of the local churchyards. The Melrose people know all this, Nick, I think their concern was the fate of Thomas. They want to know what happened to him.'

'If he had committed suicide, would he be buried in a churchyard?' I asked. 'Didn't they bury suicides at the local crossroads, with a stake through the body.'

'They did, but that was a long time ago. The practice ended in 1823. If Thomas had died in this parish, Nick, he would have been buried here – or if his body had been found on the moors or somewhere beyond our parish boundary, he'd have been brought here for burial. I'd say he perished on the moors and his body has never been found.'

'So Hester was left a widow. Who did she marry?' I asked.

'A local farmer called Sanderson. That was in 1872. He moved into the farm, then he and Hester ran it together for years, passing it down through the eldest son as is the local custom.'

'And Maud?'

'She married Henry Barr, an Elsinby farmer, in 1894. They produced a son called John in 1897; he moved to Staffordshire to work in one of the potteries and after the First World War married Hilda Craggs. Kathleen was their daughter, and she is now Mrs Melrose.'

'So the mystery is what happened to Thomas Sinclair?' I said. 'The rest seems an ordinary family story, much like any other.'

'Right, Nick.'

'So why won't the local people talk about it? Is there something they're keeping from us – some dark secret? If it was merely a case of Thomas vanishing without trace, you'd think it would still be a talking point, a thing of interest even for the present village.'

'I've not been here as long as you, Nick, so they're not likely to tell me if they won't tell you. But I know of no dark secret – and neither do the Melroses. Anyway, why are you involved? It's not a police matter, is it?'

'Pure curiosity, Christian. I like to know what is happening, and what's been happening, on my patch. If somebody's covering up something, then I want to know. Call it snooping if you like, but there is something odd about all this. I can't understand why the local folks refuse to talk about it, especially as it happened such a long time ago.'

'Perhaps it's because they don't like people snooping!' he smiled.

Following that chat with the vicar, I decided I would not spend any more of my free time trying to discover a solution to the mystery of Thomas's disappearance.

Like the other villagers, I would declare the subject closed. But like all lengthy crime enquiries, and especially murder investigations, it is often something totally disconnected which leads to a solution. In this case, it was a visit to a second-hand shop at Keswick in the Lake District.

My family and I were enjoying our summer holiday in a cottage near Ullswater and on the day – a damp and misty one – we decided to spend some time in Keswick where we could find shelter, shops and a plentiful supply of drinks and food. I found a second-hand shop full of fascinating odds and ends and, always interested in old books, I began to browse among the stock of books, magazines and prints. Hanging on the wall above me was a painting of a huge ox, with a top-hatted man standing nearby. The massive animal, a longhorn, was painted in a mixture of greyish-brown and white and had long white horns; it was a mammoth creature. At first, I did not pay a lot of attention to the picture but then, as I straightened my back after poring through some Lakeland topographical books, I noticed the caption. It said, 'The Elsinby Ox'.

Although Elsinby was a village on my beat, and only two miles from Aidensfield, I had never heard of the Elsinby Ox. Closer examination revealed a note under the caption which said the ox was born in 1840 and when it was slaughtered in 1851 following the breaking of a leg, it weighed 188 stone. So far as was known, only the famous Durham Ox, a shorthorn, was a larger beast. The painting was priced at £2. *10s. 0d.* I lifted it from the wall and upon turning it around discovered that a fairly modern newspaper clipping had been pasted to the rear of the picture.

According to the cutting, the Elsinby Ox had been reared by John and George Sinclair, farmers of Spennymoor in County Durham; they had moved to High Barns, Elsinby, a village on the North York Moors, when their ox had grown to such massive proportions that they used to transport it around for display at agricultural shows and fairs in the north-east. Later, their children, Thomas aged 15 and Hester aged 12, helped to care for the massive animal during its travels to exhibitions – it travelled in this way for just over five years before breaking a leg during a stumble in a rabbit hole. Rivalled only by the Durham Ox wich had been travelling to exhibitions earlier that century, this splendid longhorn became known as the Elsinby Ox.

And there, in this one compact note, was the reason for the reticence of the villagers of present-day Elsinby.

Thomas and Hester Sinclair were brother and sister, not man and wife. That meant that their child, Maud, was the result of incest. I began to guess that, upon the birth of the little girl, Thomas would have been condemned by the local people and so it was quite feasible that he could have committed suicide. If he had, Hester had apparently remained to face her critics and to rear the little girl. Indeed, she had eventually married a Sanderson and so her rehabilitation had been complete. Later, so it would seem, her daughter had married into a good family – the Barrs – and Mrs Melrose was a descendant. Intrigued by my good fortune, I bought the picture of the Elsinby Ox, half thinking it might be of interest to the Melrose family and half thinking it would be useful for my own collection of Yorkshire memorabilia.

Having acquired the picture, though, I was now faced with the same dilemma as the other more senior residents of Elsinby – should I tell the Melrose couple what I had discovered? Should I inform Kathleen Melrose that her grandmother was the result of an incestuous relationship between a brother and his sister? After due reflection, I decided against it. I felt it would be better if she never knew about that sordid chapter in the history of her family.

A few months later, I revisited High Barns on a routine check of stock registers and after signing the books over a nice coffee, I said to Jim, 'You know about the Elsinby Ox? And its links with your farm?'

'Aye, I do, Nick. Some animal, eh?'

I told him about my discovery in the Keswick second-hand shop, and of its revelation, adding, 'So I know there was incest, Jim. But I shan't say anything to that Melrose couple. Like you said at the time, it's best they don't know.'

He rubbed his bristly chin with a huge hand and smiled, 'Well, you're wrong, Nick. It wasn't incest. But the problem was that everybody thought it was. One of the Sandersons fathered that child, Nick, but Hester made folks think it was Thomas. They gave him a hell of a time, Nick, the local folks. Hester wasn't all that bright, you see;

she thought it better to say her brother was the dad because folks frowned on lasses having illegitimate bairns. Put up to it, she was. By the Sandersons. So Maud wasn't the result of incest, Nick. Nowt of the sort, but she was illegitimate.'

'But she married a Sanderson later, didn't she?' I asked. 'And that would legitimize the little girl?'

'Aye, it would, although she kept the Sinclair name, but it meant that yon Sanderson man got the farm. Which is what he wanted all along. He got rid of Thomas, making him an exile, so he could get his hands on the farm through Hester. Thomas, the eldest son, should have inherited the farm. He was a nasty piece of work, Nick, was that Sanderson. But if you think about it, even a chap like that would hardly marry a woman who'd committed incest, would he?'

'Do the local people know all this?'

'I doubt it,' he said. 'I should think most of them have memories of their parents, grandparents and great-grandparents talking about High Barns and the incest which made Thomas run away. Mebbe they don't know the truth of what the Sandersons did.'

'So what happened to Thomas? Was his body ever found? Did he commit suicide?'

'He knew every inch of those moors, Nick, so he'd never get lost; he never took a firearm away with him and he was made of stern stuff. He had a bit of money put away, so he took that, walked away across to the other side of the moors and caught a coach to Leicestershire. Then he worked on a farm down there, rearing his own livestock and selling it in his spare time. He bought and sold until he had enough money to set himself up on his own farm. Then he married and had a family.'

'How do you know all this?' I asked.

'Family word of mouth, Nick. He was my great-grandfather on my mother's side,' smiled Jim. 'We're back home you see, at High Barns.'

The next time I called, I presented Jim with my picture of the Elsinby Ox but even today, I do not know if the Melrose family ever discovered the truth.

* * *

The third circumstances to which I referred at the beginning of this chapter generated rather more involvement by the police and was even more traumatic for two families.

One family was called Warriner and they owned and managed a busy newsagent's in Ashfordly. Known simply as Warriners, it was just off the market place and occupied a former large stone-built house which had been converted to provide business premises on the ground floor with a flat above. The owners, Joyce and Ian Warriner, lived in a nice detached house about half a mile away, and the flat was occupied by their daughter, Tessa. Vivacious and blonde, she was in her early twenties and worked in the shop, alternating with her father to rise early to prepare the newspapers for distribution by their team of delivery boys. Apart from newspapers and magazines, they sold sweets, cigarettes, maps, stationery of various kinds, paperback books and ice cream. It was a busy shop which was popular with its customers, chiefly due to the cheerfulness of Tessa, and it provided a good living for the Warriners.

It opened at 6 a.m. which meant it attracted the early morning workers, many of whom popped in for their daily paper, cigarettes and sweets.

Lots of them bought the same things every day of the week and if Tessa or her father were working on their own, sorting the piles of newspapers for delivery, most of the regulars would help themselves to whatever they wanted and pop their money on the counter. It was that kind of shop, although when tourists and strangers walked in, there was more formality and security.

Usually, there was some good-natured banter between the customers and staff, particularly those who called in the early hours – and among them were several police officers who were working early turn. If I was working an early route on my motor bike or in the minivan with which I was later issued, I would pop into Warriners for a bar of fruit and nut chocolate or a paper to read during my meal break. In that way, I got to know Tessa and her parents quite well.

They were a very nice family – there was a son too, called Brian, but he was working away from home, something to do with the chemical industry on Teesside, and he came home for weekends. But it was Tessa who enlivened many a dull morning for those early-morning newspaper and cigarette buyers.

One of them was a man called Stuart Cabler who lived in my patch. His home was at Briggsby, a hill-top village between Aidensfield and Ashfordly, and he went to work every day on a small motor bike. He worked as a machine operator in a bacon factory at Brantsford and started work each weekday at 6.30 a.m. His journey to work took about twenty-five minutes but he allowed a little extra time for his newspaper stop in Ashfordly *en route*, and a little more time upon arrival to change from his motor-cycle gear into his work clothing.

In his early fifties, he was a small man, a mere five feet two inches tall, and correspondingly thin with a skull-like balding head adorned with thin wisps of fair hair. He had a thin fair moustache too, and matching eyebrows, and wore rounded spectacles with small lenses. For his ride to work, he dressed in an old RAF greatcoat, wellington boots, an RAF pilot's helmet and goggles.

Although meagre, his wage had enabled him to marry and he lived with his wife, Frances, in a council house in Briggsby; there were no children of the union although the couple did keep a pair of spaniels and a canary. Frances helped the family finances by working at a dairy farm in the village. They were a very quiet couple, clearly devoted to one another, and their only interests, apart from walking the dogs, appeared to be their garden and the village chapel. The garden was always beautifully maintained and spectacular with flowers from spring into late autumn; it was a veritable showpiece. Frances also kept the Methodist chapel in a clean and neat condition, both inside and out. Stuart helped with things like running repairs and decorating. Frances made sure there were always flowers inside, taking them from her own garden and, after the Sunday services, she pottered around with a duster and brush.

Every working day, therefore, Stuart left home shortly after 5.50 a.m and rode the short distance into Ashfordly where he parked his machine on its rest in the street outside Warriners. As he usually arrived a couple of minutes before the shop opened, he waited patiently and was then first into the shop when the door was opened.

Tessa, or her father, whomever was working at that time, would put out Stuart's *Daily Mirror*, packet of ten Woodbines and a Mars Bar and, upon collecting them, Stuart would place his money on the counter before bidding his farewell. It was a morning routine which never varied.

Whereas Mr Warriner would merely say 'Good morning, Mr Cabler', Tessa would show a little more friendship. She would smile at this early customer, ask him about the weather outside or praise his garden which she had noticed from time to time when passing through Briggsby. Sometimes, if he did not have the correct change, she would knock off a penny, or suggest he paid next time – and she always smiled at him. And she had such a lovely smile and a figure which was stunning. Even the loose smock she wore in the shop would not conceal her splendid shape.

Once when his motor-cycle glove had got wet after falling into a puddle as he was parking the machine, she had offered him one of her own woollen gloves to get him to work, saying he could return it in the morning. In other words, Tessa showed a range of small courtesies and oceans of smiling friendship towards Stuart Cabler and there is little doubt that these niceties brightened his day and sent him off to work whistling as he drove along the quiet road. He was just one of the many early-morning customers at Warriners but remembered by them because he was always the first to arrive.

Then Tessa began to receive obscene notes through the letterbox. Marked with her name but without the name of the writer, they arrived sometime between closing at 7.00 p.m. and reopening next morning at 6.00 a.m. In every case, they were pushed through the letterbox of the shop door. They were in small plain brown envelopes and written on lined paper, the kind one might find in a cheap school exercise book or writing pad. They were written in blue ballpoint ink in block capital letters and expressed, in no uncertain terms, what the writer would like to do to Tessa in bed, on the sofa, in the woods or elsewhere. At first, she thought they were from a schoolboy in the town, or written as some kind of crude joke and she ignored them. She never told anyone, however, but simply threw them into the wastebin.

After receiving seven or eight such letters in a period of a couple of months, the tone of the letters hardened. Instead of saying what he would like to do to Tessa, the writer threatened that he was actually going to do all the things he had mentioned and now, because she lived in the flat above the shop, she became alarmed. She told her parents and they suggested she move into their house until the letters ceased. Even at that stage, the Warriners did not inform the police, thinking the letters were the work of a crank who would soon tire of them. They did notice, however, that the letters arrived only when Tessa was working her early shift – none arrived when Mr Warriner was due to work an early shift in the shop.

But the letters did not cease. At the rate of one a week, they continued and then began to include photographs and drawings taken from obscene magazines and books, with inked-in messages saying, 'Me and You' or 'Tessa on top, me beneath' and other commentaries.

The Warriners, and Tessa in particular, had no idea who was sending these notes, nor did they know at what time they were being pushed through the letterbox. From time to time, they had kept discreet observations upon their premises, but without any success. Mr Warriner had offered to work every early-morning shift but Tessa had said she did not want this nut-case to ruin her life or change the family routine.

It was when used contraceptives were included in the envelopes that the Warriners contacted Ashfordly Police. Not every one included this extra item but it was the first of such packages which prompted Mr Warriner to inform Sergeant Blaketon. It was then that the entire story emerged, with Tessa saying she had no idea of the identity of the sender. She had never given any encouragement to anyone visiting the shop, nor had any of her customers given any indication they might have had that kind of romantic notion towards her. The identity of her unbalanced admirer was a mystery.

Sergeant Blaketon told the family that the only way to catch the offending person was for a police officer to be concealed on the premises to watch for the arrival of the letters. It was thought they were coming after midnight when the town was quiet – one or other of the Warriner family was usually on the premises until 9 p.m. even though the shop was closed. Another theory was that the letters arrived in the very early hours of the morning, before the shop opened. The family had, for a time, maintained a vigil without any success.

One or other of the family was usually in the shop around 5.30 a.m. as the papers were delivered from the wholesaler but because they were invariably sorting them in the rear room, they could not constantly watch the letterbox at the front. The delivery van dropped the papers at the rear door, which was the door the staff used to enter the premises prior to opening of the public. And, they said, they did not always go through the shop to the front door immediately upon arriving at 5.30 a.m., so they could not say whether the letters came during the night or early in the morning. But, quite often when going to open up for the day, the buff envelope addressed to Tessa would be lying on the mat.

The snag was that the letters did not arrive in a regular pattern. They might arrive on a Wednesday morning one week, a Tuesday the next, then a Friday or even a Sunday on some occasions. There was not always a letter each week – some weeks, two arrived, and during other weeks, none. There was no discernible pattern, which made police observations rather difficult and time-consuming.

One problem from the official police aspect was that the offender was not committing a crime – there was no statute by which his behaviour was punishable in a court of law which meant that long hours of silent observations by the police might be difficult to justify. The only thing we might do, if we caught him, was to arrest him for conduct which was likely to cause a breach of the peace, and present him before the magistrates' court to have him bound over to be of good behaviour.

Catching him was important, but that presented the problem. Could we justify a continuing police presence in the shop when there was other work to consider? But as time went by, Tessa did begin to feel the strain. She felt she was under constant observation although no one had been observed hanging around the premises, and yet, bravely, she continued with her normal routine. Happily, the unwelcome attention she was receiving did not progress to telephone calls but Sergeant Blaketon, justifying his actions as being necessary for her safety, did initiate a system of observations by police officers of the Ashfordly section. And that included me.

As my turn came when the nights and mornings were brightening with a new spring, I had to enter the shop at 10 p.m. under the cover of darkness and via the rear door, and remain there until it opened at 6 a.m. Mr Warriner showed me the kettle and coffee, and positioned a chair at the back of the shop, in the darkness, from where I could watch the front door all through the night. It was agreed that the front door would be unlocked while I was watching it, so that I could gallop out in rapid pursuit of the villain if he turned up. It would be a long and dreary vigil and I had no hope of catching the offender. He – (or could it be a she with a vengeance?) – seemed to arrive when no one was maintaining such observations.

Shortly after ten o'clock one Tuesday night, therefore, I settled upon the hard chair in the darkness of the shop to begin my vigil. I had a clear view of the door. Through its glass, and the glass of the shop windows, I could see the street outside which was bathed in the orange glow of the street lights and beyond was the road leading to the marketplace. Quite a lot of people were walking around at that time of night, going to or coming from the local pubs or just walking in the fresh air. An hour passed very quickly and then, a few minutes after eleven, I saw a dark figure heading for the shop doorway. It was a small person, a man by the look of it; he was wearing a long topcoat whose colour I could not discern in the dim light but he wore glasses which glinted in the reflected beams of the street lamps. He was scurrying towards the shop ... quickly, I got up from my chair. I must not reveal my presence, but knew that the layout of the shop and its shelves concealed me very well from the exterior. And then he came right to the door. I heard the crash of the flap of the letter box as the man turned and hurried away. I leapt into action. As I reached the doorway, I picked up the letter and thrust it into my pocket as I followed him into the market place, without once losing sight of him. I must not lose him – I needed a continuity of evidence if I was to prove that he was the phantom postman.

As I hurried into the market place, I saw him board a service bus – the last bus from Ashfordly to Galtreford via Briggsby, Aidensfield and Elsinby. I climbed aboard just as he was taking his seat and, as he turned to face me, I saw it was Stuart Cabler. His specs and his long RAF greatcoat gave him away. I asked him to leave the bus because I wanted to talk to him, and he followed me without a word. I led him back to the shop, the door being unlocked, and took him inside where I switched on the lights. I then produced the envelope from my pocket and showed it to him.

'I was inside the shop, Mr Cabler, and I saw you deliver this letter, addressed to Tessa. Did you deliver it a few minutes ago?'

He flushed deeply and whispered hoarsely. 'Yes. It's ... it's my paper money ... to pay the bill....'

I opened it. It contained a used contraceptive wrapped in a piece of toilet tissue and a foul, obscene note written in blue ballpoint in capital letters upon a piece of lined writing paper.

'A funny way of paying your paper bill, Mr Cabler,' I said. 'You know that there have been lots of these letters, so we can compare the handwriting on them all, now that you have admitted delivering this one.'

'I'm sorry,' was all he said. 'I am so dreadfully sorry ... I did not want to frighten her. I do not know why I did it....'

I took him to the police station where Sergeant Blaketon explained that he would be bailed to appear at Eltering Magistrates' Court on Friday, when an application would be made to have him bound over to keep the peace or to be of good behaviour. He told us he travelled from Briggsby into Ashfordly by the last bus – it halted in the market place for twenty minutes to collect people leaving the pubs, and then returned to Galtreford. In that way, Stuart Cabler would be away from home for only half an hour, having told his wife he was going for a walk before going to bed. Having put the miserable little man through the official procedures, Sergeant Blaketon offered to run him home as I went to inform the Warriners of our modest success, but Cabler said he would take a taxi.

He offered no reason for his bizarre behaviour, and when I told the Warriners, they were shocked and surprised, Tessa saying she had never knowingly given him any encouragement. But clearly, over the months, he had developed an obsession with the pretty young woman and this was his odd way of showing his desire for her.

Stuart Cabler did not go into the shop the following morning, even though Tessa had put out his *Daily Mirror*, Woodbines and Mars Bar, and he did not turn up for work either. It was around noon that a forestry worker rang Ashfordly Police to say he had found the body of a man hanging from a tree in Hagg End Wood. It was Stuart Cabler, but he had not left a note.

Those who knew him, and the wife who loved him devotedly, were devastated by his sudden suicide, none of them knowing about his recent arrest and the reason for it, and the coroner felt he could deliver his verdict without referring to that aspect of Cabler's life.

And so no one told his wife about his sordid activities. The Warriners agreed they would not tell Mrs Cabler, nor anyone else, about the obscene letters or the man who had sent them. There are times when I wonder if Mrs Cabler should have been told, or whether it is better for loved ones to remain ignorant of certain matters relating to their spouses or family members. Sadly, there is no simple answer to that problem.

9

'The Lord shall join his enemies together.'

Isa. 9.11

In the North York Moors during the early years of this century, Catholics and Protestants kept a discreet and respectful distance from one another. They went their separate ways to church; Catholics tended to marry Catholics, go to Catholic schools and avoid Protestant services like the plague. Even in the 1960s, the moorland Catholics, whose faith had survived the Reformation and produced at least one martyr, were smarting from the wholesale confiscation of their churches by the state, losing to the Protestants hundreds of gems like York Minster and Westminster Abbey. Then there was the sad matter of the wholesale destruction of their abbeys, priories and monasteries in the sixteenth and seventeenth centuries.

But after the Penal Times, the climate began to thaw. The Catholic Emancipation Act was passed in 1829 to allow their limited return to British society – they could once more hold commissions in the armed forces, attend university, inherit land and serve with the judiciary, although they couldn't marry the sovereign or become prime minister. They also set about building new churches.

Protestants belonging to the Church of England, on the

other hand, were far more open in their faith; they would marry into other churches without any of the trauma suffered by their Catholic friends, and most couldn't understand what the fuss was about, even though many regarded themselves as the true Catholics of this country.

With Aidensfield being a predominantly Catholic village, the differences in Catholic and Protestant belief led to many long discussions in the pubs and houses of Aidensfield and district. But these were friendly and warm, and real anger rarely ensued.

But in more recent times, further conciliatory moves were afoot. In 1962, Pope John XXIII opened the now famous council known as Vatican II, and this was attended by observers fron non-Catholic churches throughout the word. That, in itself, was a major step towards church unity. Vatican II – opened in 1962 and concluded in December 1965 – concerned itself with changes to the liturgy, Christian unity and matters of church governments throughout the world.

One major outcome of those deliberations was the joining together of the Catholic and Anglican churches of Aidensfield in a garden fête. As a move towards Christian unity, this was regarded as having much greater significance than any Vatican Council, Church of England Synod or even the World Council of Churches.

I am not sure how the idea started but one Sunday in March, The Reverend Christian Lord of the Anglican Church of All Saints and Father Adrian of St Aidan's Catholic Church simultaneously announced from their pulpits that there should be a joint garden fête. Its objective was to bring together members of each congregation in a friendly manner, a supplementary purpose being to raise funds for each church and for local charities. A committee comprising members from each church would be set up to run the fête, the date of which was the final Saturday in August, and it was hoped it would create a new feeling of unity within Aidensfield.

Fr Adrian rang me later that Sunday to ask if I would be a member of that committee and although I do not like them (I am of the firm belief that a camel is a horse which was designed by a committee), I agreed. The chairman, he added, would be a man called Rupert Brown, an avowed atheist. It was felt he would not take sides should there be a dispute. The secretary would be Miss Protheroe from All Saints, and the treasurer would be Mrs Carstairs from St Aidan's. A nice balance of officials, I felt.

The first meeting was a fortnight later and I went along to the committee room of the village hall – neutral ground, I was pleased to note – to join the others. There were some fifteen people in the room representing various aspects of village life, such as the two schools, the churches, the Womens' Institute, Catholic Womens' League, cricket club, football club, the pubs and other local groups and societies. I realized I was there partly because I attended the Catholic church, but also because of my job. A policeman on such a committee is often thought to be a good idea, if only that it will ensure his uniformed presence on the day, along with his professional expertise in acquiring things like No Parking signs, loudhailers and free offers of displays from the crime prevention teams

'Right,' said Mr Brown, opening the meeting. 'This is the first meeting of the Anglican and Catholic churches garden fête committee....'

'No,' said someone at the far end of the table. 'It's surely the Catholic and Anglican churches garden fête committee ... Catholics were here a thousand years before the Protestants, they have priority.'

'It should be St Aidan's and All Saints Churches Fête,' put in another woman.

I spoke up now. 'Why don't we just call it the Aidensfield Churches Garden Fête? Churches in the plural, it includes everyone, and then the Methodists and Quakers won't feel left out.'

'A good idea,' beamed Mr Brown. 'All in agreement?'

After this initial sparring and flurry of partisan spirits, things settled down and the committee set about its task of organizing the fête. One of the first problems was a suitable site. In order not to show preference to either church, a garden belonging to an independent person would be ideal, but of the two village gardens which were large enough to accommodate the proposed fête, one belonged to a Catholic and the other to an Anglican. There were plenty of suitable fields around the village, their ownership being spread among the differing faiths in a fairly even way, but it was then decided that the best place would be the village green.

It had been used for communal gatherings in the past, and it was representative of the entire village. This was an eminently suitable and independent site which meant that the title of the event could not include the word 'garden'. That was therefore dropped with little ceremony and the newly-styled village fête would comprise stalls showing local handicrafts, a section for vegetable and flower shows, a contest for beautiful dogs, cats and other pets, displays of sheepdogs at work, a donkey race, a cake stall, coconut shy, games for adults and children, a bar, a brass band playing throughout the afternoon, art and handwriting competitions and sundry other events of considerable variety and range.

It was suggested that the local quoits teams and cricket teams might play exhibition matches, that there be contests such as sack-races, three-legged races, egg-and-spoon races, long jumps and high jumps for children, and that swings, roundabouts and slides be brought in for the infants to use.

Over the weeks, those ideas, with a few more added, became realities. Marquees and tents were booked, pitches reserved, sites established for the stalls and a sports arena, car-parking arrangements made, a first-aid tent selected and a draft programme produced. I had arranged to be on duty in Aidensfield that day, and there is little doubt that the committee was doing a good job. Things were happening, there was a positive air about the place, and then, at one of the committee meetings, Rory O'Brien, an Irishman living in Aidensfield, said, 'Mr Chairman, an idea.'

'Yes, Mr O'Brien?' Rory was known as a Big Catholic because he never missed mass, rang the bell, took the collection and cut the lawns around St Aidans. For some obscure reason, Catholics who were openly keen on their faith were called Big Catholics, which had nothing to do with their physical atttributes. There were a lot of Big Catholics in Aidensfield. In Rory's case, he was in his late forties, a successful businessman with interests in building, horse racing and two seaside restaurants.

'We have lots of sports organized for the fête – children and adults – quoits and cricket matches, races and things,' said Rory O'Brien.

'We have indeed,' said Mr Brown.

'Would it not be an idea to have a competition between the two churches?'

Mr Brown, an atheist, pursed his lips and said, 'I thought the idea of this fête was to eliminante competition between the churches? To bring them together, to fuse them into one happy Christian unit?'

'To be sure it will do that, Mr Chairman, but I was thinking of the sports. A sports competition. Competition is good for the soul. So why not a cricket team from All Saints playing a team from St Aidan's? To add a bit of excitement to the days events. And the same with the quoits team. And even the children – a sack race between the two schools, Catholic and Protestant....'

'Well, I am not sure ...' began Mr Brown, sensing this could produce discord and trouble at the very time conciliatory moves were required.

'I'll give a cup to the winning church,' continued O'Brien unabashed. 'The Aidensfield Churches Fête Cup, to be presented annually. And a cheque for five hundred pounds.'

I was sure it was the reference to a cheque which transformed the concept of this suggestion.

'And how would you determine the winner?' I asked, as a representative of each church licked their lips at the thought of a £500 donation.

'Each team and each individual would score one point for a win. So if St Aidan's won the cricket match, they'd earn one point. But if little Johnny Swinton won his sack race for All Saints' School, he'd score one point for the Anglicans. And if Margaret Tulley won the egg-and-spoon race for St Aidan's School, that would be a point for the

Catholic church. An odd number of qualifying events would produce a clear winner without the chance of a draw occurring. And at the end of the day, we add the points to see who'd got the prize. It's a bit of fun, nothing more than a bit of extra excitement throughout the day, and a means for one of the churches to get a useful contribution to its funds.'

There was a moment of silence as the committee considered this suggestion, then one of them said, 'I see no harm in it, Mr Brown. There's always been healthy competition in these moors, especially between village cricket and quoits teams; even though the teams beat each other soundly, they remain the best of friends. In this case, the same people will be playing, but they'll be representing a church team instead of a village team. After all, they're used to one another, our teams have always consisted of a healthy mixture of Catholics and Protestants. This time they'll be playing for God, not their village. I think it's a good idea.'

'I'm sure the spirit of the occasion will keep things calm and measured,' I offered.

'They're not going to fall out over a cricket match at a church fête! I would support the idea,' put in another of the committee members.

That speech led to mutterings of agreement among the othes and I found myself unable to think of a reason why the plan would cause trouble. And so it was agreed. It was then suggested that panels to record the on-going scores should be printed in the fête programme.

The next task was to circulate that decision to the villagers, sports clubs and schools, so that teams could be recruited and there is no doubt that the promise of a handsome cup and a big cheque did enliven the planning of the fête. Quite suddenly, there was talk of 'winning the cup' and what had been planned as a simple fête had now assumed the status of a major sporting event along the lines of the FA Cup Final. I began to wonder if I'd need more no-parking signs and a more sonorous loudhailer.

The arrangements went ahead with remarkable speed and flair until, a few days before the fête, Aidensfield village green was transformed. Marquees and tents, cattle pens and rabbit hutches, stalls and tables, swings and roundabouts, notices and turnstiles, white lines and no-parking signs all appeared and then on a brilliant sunny day with not a cloud in the sky, the Aidensfield Churches Fête opened to music, noise, cars, buses, crowds and happiness.

Most of us had a role to play and, in the initial stages at least, mine was to ensure that all the incoming cars and buses found a parking space and that the road through the village was not obstructed. There was a very hectic period of about three-quarters of an hour – everyone seemed to arrive at the same time and then, once the opening cermeony had been concluded, my duties relaxed as people wandered about, visiting each stall or display in turn. And I did likewise.

There was an excellent turnout with people coming from the villages and hamlets which surrounded Aidensfield, part of this being due, I felt, to the sporting atmosphere which had been generated.

There was even talk of bookmakers operating during the fête, with betting on the outcome of the individual or combined sporting events, including the egg-and-spoon race and other children's races. But I chose to ignore that possibility – if there was a bookmaker at the fête, his or her activities would be illegal in these circumstances, so it was best I knew nothing about it. I did not want the happy occasion to be ruined by having to prosecute the committee for allowing unlawful betting on the village green.

As I patrolled among the stalls and displays, the cricket and quoits matches were being played, with St Aidan's batting first in the cricket match and All Saints ahead in the quoits. With St Aidan's winning some events and All Saints the others, most of the earlier events meant that the scores were fairly level throughout the afternoon. The mums competed in the hundred yards, the relay, an hilarious egg-and-spoon race and a sack race while dads did the high jump, long jump, a relay and throwing the cricket ball. By the time the cricket and quoits matches

halted for tea, St Aidan's had scored 10 points and All
Saint's 11. The cricket and quoits resumed as the
children's events got underway and it was becoming clear
that the winner of the cup would almost certainly be
decided by the children's competitions. There were a lot of
races which were to be arranged in heats prior to the finals
and it was decided that there would be a point for the
winner of each heat, as well as one for the winner of each
final, but always with an odd number of events to
guarantee an outright winner.

I wandered among the crowds, sometimes having to
carry a wandering toddler to the lost children tent or
provide first aid to someone who had trapped their finger
in the turnstile or banged their head on a tent pole but it
was an unexciting time. From time to time, cheers rose
above the noise of the crowds as a cricketer took a wicket
or scored a run, and then I realized that the scores for each
church were even – and it was that which was causing the
excitement. St Aidan's had scored 128 all out in the cricket
match, and now All Saints were 118 with two wickets in
hand, hence the tension. All Saints had won the quoits
match, I was told, and as I moved towards the sports field,
I saw that the overall score was: All Saints 18, St Aidan's
17. It was all to play for – and the only events to complete
were the cildren's sports. And then a wicket tumbled in
the cricket match.

All Saints were 122 for 9, with the last man coming in to
bat but with a wild swing, known locally as a cow swipe,
with which he hoped he would score a six; he missed and
was clean bowled. St Aidan's had won the cricket. The
total score was 18 for each church.

It meant that everything depended upon the children
and part of the day's achievement was to make sure that
every child entered at least one of the contests. St Aidan's
won the under-5s sprint for girls and the under 10s
egg-and-spoon race for boys; then All Saints drew ahead
with cracking wins in the 5-8s boys sack race, the 8-10s
long jump for boys and the girls 15-18s hundred yard race.

The tension and interest thus created was quite
astonishing and there is little doubt that the competitors,

young as they were, entered their races with the fervour of missionaries. Cheers rent the air as successive teams assembled and tore towards the finishing lines, with roars of approval or cries of dismay, dependant upon whom one was supporting as the winning line was crossed.

And quite suddenly, it was over. The score was 27 each – but there should have been a clear winner, and there wasn't. There was a frantic check of the completed events when it was revealed that the organizers had omitted one of the races. With everything to play for, there was a further race to be completed but no one knew which had been omitted because one or two had been run simultaneously at different locations. To keep the tension high, the announcer said,

'Ladies and gentlemen. There is one more race – the decider for the Aidensfield Churches Challenge Cup. It will begin in five minutes. The winner will ensure that a fine Challenge Cup and a cheque for £500 goes to the winning church – and what a climax this will be! Be there – see the cliff-hanging climax in five minutes....'

There was then a frantic check of the list to see which race had been omitted and it was shown to be the 5-8s three-legged race for boys. Somehow, the race organizers had overlooked it on the long list of events, but it meant that the honour of winning the cup now rested upon the competitors in this final test, a band of tiny lads.

The announcer called for the youngsters to assemble at the starting point but some had wandered off, thinking they would not be called to race or believing that they had perhaps not heard an earlier call. And so there was something of a scramble to persuade parents to ensure their children were ready. Eventually, with the entire crowd assembled around the arena, the lads were gathered together, with each school being well represented. It was then that I noticed two lads walking towards the arena – I knew one as Brendan O'Ryan, aged 7, because he had once had his bicycle stolen from outside St Aidan's school, but I did not know the other.

'Come on, you two!' I shouted. 'You're just in time for the big race! Where have you been?'

'We've just come, Mr Rhea,' said Brendan. 'Dad had to go to Scarborough.'

'Well, you're just in time. So who is this?' I asked the other boy.

'Timothy Riley,' said the other one.

'How old are you, Timothy?' I asked him.

'Seven,' he said.

'And you are Brendan's friend?'

'No, he's my cousin,' said Brendan.

'Right, get up to the start of the three-legged race, have your legs tied together and run for your lives when the whistle goes. Can you do that?'

'Yes, Mr Rhea,' said Brendan.

'Yes, sir,' echoed Timothy

As the boys hurried to the starting point for an official to tie a duster around their ankles in a regulation knot, I saw Brendan's mother and father heading towards me and thought they should be told where the boys were. Mr O'Ryan said he'd had some important business which had taken longer than he'd expected, and was sorry he had missed the fun of the fête, but was delighted to see Brendan and his cousin preparing for the three-legged race. I wondered if the O'Ryans realized how much was riding upon the back of each pair of children in this race, but they seemed not to have appreciated the tension into which they had just walked.

Then the starter shouted, 'Ready, everyone?' A hush descended upon the gatherng. 'Children?'

A row of boys, each with one leg tied to that of a friend, stood at the starting point with one of their arms around the back of their partner. All were staring intently at the finishing tape. The starter shouted, 'Right. When I shout Go – run for that tape....' There was a pause as the crowd lapsed into a respectful silence and then we heard the starter call, 'Ready, steady – Go!'

A roar filled the air as hundreds of voices cheered on the galloping lads and then I saw the O'Ryan and Riley twosome gain a very useful lead. They were running with practised skill, the rhythm of their movements taking them well ahead of their competitors and they crossed the finishing line well ahead of anyone else to the rousing cheers of the St Aidan supporters.

The announcer, with a microphone in his hands, went up to Brendan and Timothy as they were removing their bond and I heard him say, 'Brendan, which is your school?'

'St Aidan's, the Catholic school sir,' he said quietly, as the place erupted into cheers as the assembled Catholics realized their church would get the £500 and the cup.

But then we heard the amplified voice of Timothy say, 'But I'm starting at All Saints on Monday.'

The cheers died away as the announcer said, 'You are new here?'

'Yes, sir, I'm staying with my aunt and uncle until Mum and Dad move house. I am not a Catholic, so I will go to All Saints Primary.'

And there was a roar from All Saints' supporters as the announcer said, 'Well, I declare the result to be an admirable draw! The cup will be held by each church for six months and the cash prize divided between the two. A very worthy result if I may so so.'

And so it was. St Sebastian, the patron saint of athletes would have been well pleased.

There is little doubt that the success of the joint churches fête was responsible for a softening of attitudes between the congregations, but another conciliatory event swiftly followed.

Due to dwindling congregations, one of the two Methodist chapels in Aidensfield had closed a few years earlier and it had remained untouched and unused.

A handsome building constructed of local moorland granite, it was full of rich woodwork; it had been built in the early years of the last century on the heather-covered slopes of a steep incline overlooking the river. It was a picturesque site by any standards and several entrepreneurial builders had made approaches to purchase the old chapel with a view to converting it into a dwelling house. All had been refused permission to buy it, one reason being that the reduction of numbers might be of a temporary nature, and that an upsurge of interest in Methodism was anticipated. But that renewal of faith never happened and the old chapel became more and more dilapidated in appearance.

It was therefore decided, with some reluctance, that the old chapel should be sold and so it was put on the market. It was quickly purchased for a very reasonable price by a local builder called Duncan Goodwin. He wasted no time in gutting the place, selling off the benches and stripping all the beautiful timber which had remained in surprisingly good condition. In a remarkably short time, the place was a mere shell comprising little more than four stone walls and a roof as Goodwin set about his task of converting it into a modern and fahionable house with stunning views over the river and moors. He dressed the shell of the old chapel in a coat of scaffolding, re-pointed the walls, repaired the roof and prepared to instal the necessary services. From time to time as I passed I would pop in to see how things were progressing.

My visits were not connected in any way with my police work, but merely the curiosity of a village resident who felt he might like to buy the finished house. But that was an impossible dream for me – such properties were far beyond my modest salary, even if I had been allowed to buy my own home. My house came with the job! It was during one of these nosy visits that he showed me something which was to prove of immense interest.

As I entered the dusty, empty building, Duncan and his three men were taking up the floorboards. There was a bewildering amount of dust in the air as they prised the long, strong boards from the underlying beams which supported them. They were careful not to damage the woodwork because it was going to be relaid as the new floor. It was in exquisite condition, a tribute to the care lavished upon it over the years by successive chapel congregations. As I passed the time of day with Duncan, one of his men, Harry, shouted, 'Boss, here, look at this!'

Duncan, a small stocky man in his late forties, went over to Harry who had found a large hole beneath the floor.

'What is it, Harry? A well or summat?'

'It looks bigger than a well to me, more like a pit shaft.'

'We need a torch,' said Duncan.

'I've got one in my van,' I offered, and went out for it. When I returned, I found myself looking into a black and very spacious hole directly beneath the floor; I poked my torch into it and shone the light around – it looked like a room because there were walls and a floor below and I could see that the beams of the chapel floor spanned the huge gap beneath and served as a roof to the hidden room.

'Have a look.' I handed the torch to Duncan, and he passed it to the others, after which Duncan said, 'It looks like a cellar to me.'

He ordered his men to lift several more floorboards which they now did with extreme care and, as each board, some twelve inches wide, came up, it revealed more of the emptiness beneath. My torch revealed more of the old cellar, its floor covered in thick dust with pieces of large stone and other unidentified artefacts lying around. It had been undisturbed for years.

'It is a cellar,' said Duncan eventually. 'See, it's got a stone floor, good solid stone walls and there, under the far end of the chapel, there's a stone staircase rising up to our level … it's been blocked off, though. The floorboards cover the exit into the chapel.'

He was right. At the point where the staircase would have entered the chapel, the floorboards spanned the area, yet there was no indication from within the chapel that a flight of steps descended beneath it at that point. Certainly, there was no cellar flap to permit entry to the staircase and cellar below.

'So the entire chapel is standing on top of a cellar?' I said. 'It's a wonder it was never used, it would have made a massive and very useful storeroom.'

'It's funny, is that,' said Duncan. 'But if my knowledge is owt like right, those cellar walls are far older than the chapel. And see, at the front....' He was guiding the beam of my torch around the walls beneath.

'Overlooking the beck?' I said.

'Aye, there's been a window there, it's blocked up now.

With matching stone ... it's been a church window, I reckon, Mr Rhea, see its outline?'

He was right. The shape of the blocked-up window was just like those of the parish church – a tall, narrow shape rounded at the top before coming to a point. And there were similar windows at each side too, close to the one which overlooked the river. All were blocked with stone.

'But you can't see the outline of those windows from the outside, can you?' I asked.

'It's all overgrown down there, Mr Rhea, briars and rubbish. It's been like that for as long as I can remember. You can't really get close to that cellar wall at the outside, it's become part of the cliff in that gully. From the far side of the beck, this wall now looks like part of the chapel. Looking at it more carefully, you could think it had been built years ago, long before the chapel, mebbe to stop landslides, then used to support the chapel.'

'You're saying those cellar walls could have been there for centuries? What's the history of the chapel site, Duncan, any idea?'

'Not really. When I bought the spot, I found there'd been a barn here before the chapel was built – some farmer let the Methodists have the barn so they could put a chapel here but I've no idea what the barn looked like. The chapel was built in 1812-1813, but I have no idea how long the old barn had been there before that or whether the walls of the barn were re-used to make the chapel.'

'There's nothing in the history of the village to say there'd ever been a church on this site, is there?' I asked.

'Nay, Mr Rhea, I'm no historian. But I never saw owt about an old church when I was buying the spot, and the planning committee never mentioned it. So far as I knew, this had been a barn for years and years, and then a chapel, and I got permission to change it into a dwelling house. You don't think this cellar's from an old church, do you?'

'It looks like a crypt,' I said. 'I don't know much about such things but it's very like that crypt at Lastingham, isn't it?'

'Lastingham? I've never seen that 'un, Mr Rhea.'

I told him about the remarkable crypt which lies beneath St Mary's Anglican Church at Lastingham in the depths of the North York Moors. Dating from Norman times, it is an entire church in its own right, complete with nave, chancel and two side aisles, and it is one of the few apsidal crypts in this country. It contains the remains of an altar and some stone crosses dating variously from the time of the Angles, the Vikings and the Danes; it is also thought to be built over the tomb of Saint Cedd, standing as it does on the site of his first monastery. Access to the crypt is through the present parish church and down a staircase through an opening in the aisle. From my memory of that old crypt, this supposed cellar looked remarkably similar.

'Does this mean I'll have to stop my conversion work?' asked Duncan.

'I doubt if anyone could compel you to stop,' I suggested. 'It's not as if you've discovered a body or a piece of gold which is subjected to the laws of treasure trove. But I would imagine that historians and archaeologists would like to examine this place before you decide what to do with it.'

'Now I know what those builders feel like as they uncover Roman remains every time they dig a street up in York!' he grinned. 'What shall I do, Mr Rhea? I mean, if this is important to the history of Aidensfield, I don't want to be responsible for ruining it.'

'I'll have a word with Tony Lyddington,' I told him.

Tony was a professional archaeologist who lived in Elsinby and he was an expert in the history of the locality; he'd be ideal.

'Shall I stop the lads?' asked Duncan warily.

'That's up to you, Duncan,' I said. 'But I can't see how they can harm the crypt while they're working on the top. Your problems might start if this is extremely old and very historic...!'

'I've other projects lined up,' he said with a shrug of his shoulders. 'We're doing this up between jobs, I can easily stop if I have to.'

I asked Duncan and his workmen not to mention this

discovery until Lyddington arrived to determine its age and former use. It would be four or five days later when Tony Lyddington found the time to visit the old chapel; he rang me to tell me the time of his proposed visit and, as I was off duty, I went along.

Duncan and his men had removed all the floorboards by this time and were busy pointing the internal walls prior to replastering. The floor supports were all in position, with a few floorboards and additional planks lying on top to provide walkways above the gaping hole beneath; now, though, the stairs into the crypt were accessible and in the crypt Duncan had rigged up an electric light bulb at the end of a long cable.

Tony Lyddington was a strange individual with long brown hair in a pony tail and he dressed in highly coloured woollen clothes, often with a woolly hat on his head and climbing boots on his feet. In his mid-forties, he was widely acknowledged as an authority on the Roman settlements of Yorkshire, with an accompanying wide knowledge of other eras. I stood to one side as Tony, from a vantage point in the chapel itself, first examined the hollow beneath the chapel and then descended via the old stone steps. He moved towards the walls, peering closely at them, and with even more closeness, studied the blocked-up windows. He ran his fingers through the dust on the floor, looked at the bits of discarded stone and then asked if there was any way he could examine the exterior. It was possible, Duncan told him, to scramble down the rocky slope outside if one held on to trees and bushes.

Eventually, he returned and smiled.

'I am almost certain it is a crypt,' he said. 'They were sometimes built on sloping sites like this, to support the church above. There's one at Shillington in Bedfordshire, I believe, but they are considerably rarer in village parish churches, particularly in the north of England. Now, I do know that there was the hint of a crypt beneath a church in Aidensfield in the thirteenth century, but all detailed records have vanished. At the time of the persecution of the Catholics in the sixteenth and seventeenth centuries, there were stories of priests coming into the country from

France, as missionaries, and hiding in the big houses of the area, then saying mass in secret. This is probably one of the places where mass was said, with secret access through the barn which used to stand here. A perfect place but due to its secrecy, one which has faded from the historic records of the area.'

'There seems to be some damage,' I pointed to the fallen pillars which still lay on the floor.

'The Normans had pillars like this, in their crypts,' he said. 'But these might have been knocked down when the floor of the chapel was laid. I'm surprised the chapel builders did not publicize the crypt.'

'If the workmen were Catholics,' I said, 'perhaps they wanted to keep the old crypt hidden, as their forefathers had done?'

'That wouldn't be too difficult,' Tony admitted. 'You just keep people out of the barn or chapel during construction by saying it's too dangerous to come in … but this is a very exciting find, Mr Goodwin. So what are you going to do with it?'

'If it was a cellar, I'd make sure it was incorporated in the house,' he said. 'but summat as historic as this, well, I don't know what to do.'

'Lots of houses in these parts have pre-Reformation chapels and other portions built into them. They're part of our Catholic heritage. It is your property, Mr Goodwin, and I doubt if anyone could compel you to retain this, or to give up your building alterations.'

'If I was to get my money back, I'd happily hand it over to the authorities,' said Duncan Goodwin. 'They might convert it into a youth club, somewhere for the kids to come on a night; with that crypt downstairs and all this space upstairs, it would make a smashing youth club or social centre.'

'Would you like me to generate some publicity on those lines?' asked Lyddington.

'Aye, why not?' grinned Duncan.

And so the story of the Aidensfield Crypt was featured in the local papers along with photographs and line drawings of what it must have been like during its use as a modest church. Several local businessmen, along with the bishop of the Catholic diocese at Middlesbrough and the Archbishop of York, joined forces to raise enough money to buy the property from Duncan, and then have it converted into a social centre for the entire village. The crypt is now part of that centre, with access via that ancient stone staircase. The blocked-up windows have been re-opened and glazed, the dirt on the floor removed, and the entire crypt sympathetically restored. A committee comprising representatives from all the churches in the village, and various other organizations, was formed, a table tennis table was installed at one end and a juke box was positioned at the other.

I'm not sure whether the saints of old would have approved of the music, but it did get the youngsters of Aidensfield off the street. And for a village policeman, that is a very worthy and useful thing to do! There were one or two questions about whether it was proper for something which had once been a church, albeit many centuries ago, to be used for secular purposes; Tony recalled the case when the Knights Templar were disbanded and the question arose about what should happen to their lands. A suitably religious purpose had to be found, and so they were given to the Knights Hospitallers of Jerusalem, but such transfers were no longer essential. So long as the church had been deconsecrated, it could be used for non-religious purposes.

And The Crypt, as it became widely known? It is still the focus for the young people of the area and the older residents welcome its presence because it keeps all the noise of strident pop music away from the village.

10

'Thou that abhorrest idols, dost thou commit sacrilege?'

Rom 2.22

To my knowledge, the above reference to sacrilege is the only time the word occurs in the Bible but it must be taken in the context in which St Paul used it. He was asking whether those who taught others had first taught themselves about the subject in which they professed to be an expert, or whether those who said it was wrong to steal actually themselves stole things. He went on to ask whether the man who said it was wrong to commit adultery would himself commit adultery and finally asked whether those who hated idols would themselves commit sacrilege. In short, and to use a modern term, St Paul says we should practise what we preach!

I am not sure what the word 'sacrilege' meant in his time, but in English law and thus for the constabularies of England and Wales, it was the name given to a crime with ecclesiastical links. It remained on the statute book until 1968 when it was replaced by burglary. Of all the crimes that could be committed with particular reference to churches, sacrilege was the one which most frequently presented operational police officers with procedural problems.

There were other church-orientated offences – blasphemy was the use of language which vilified either the Christian faith of the Bible, particularly if the language used was obscene or indecent. Dating from the twelfth century, it was the crime of attacking Christianity and bringing it into contempt, or attempting to corrupt public morale, or to shock and insult believers.

Throughout my police service, I never personally encountered a prosecution for blasphemy, a common law offence, even though I have heard some tasteless and obnoxious references to God and his church. So far as I know, the only prosecutions this century in Britain occurred in 1921 and again in 1977.

Another ecclesiastical offence which most police officers can remember from their days at training school was known as 'brawling in a churchyard'. Claude Jeremiah Greengrass was convicted of this offence in 1960, which was before my arrival at Aidensfield, but whenever I quizzed him about precisely what he had done to acquire such a conviction, he refused to enlighten me. The brawling offence could be prosecuted under the Ecclesiastical Courts Jurisdiction Act of 1860 and the offender could be arrested by either a constable or a church warden. This covered riotous, violent or indecent behaviour in any place of religious worship at any time, or in any churchyard or burial ground. A similar offence involved any wilful and malicious or contemptuous disturbance of persons assembled for religious worship, or any interference with the person officiating or of any of those assembled.

Clergymen were protected too. It was an offence to obstruct, prevent or endeavour to obstruct or prevent any clergyman from celebrating divine service or officiating in a divine service or at a funeral. Likewise, violence towards the clergy while officiating in their duties was outlawed, as was any molestation or disturbance of a clergyman during his official duties, whether in church or chapel or at a burial ground.

Bigamy might also be described as an offence against religion, although marriage is now a civil contract as well as a religious ceremony. This is the crime committed when a person who is legally married goes through a lawful form of marriage during the life of the former husband or wife. It has been described as 'an outrage against public decency', and the criminal law of this country has long regarded it as a very serious crime. A standing joke among police officers is that the penalty for committing bigamy is two mothers-in-law.

There are many other offences which specifically involve the clergy during the practice of their duties, but few, if any, are of interest to the police. But beyond all doubt, the most common offence dealt with by the police specifically so far as churches were concerned, was sacrilege. Stripping lead from church roofs was not regarded as sacrilege, however, because the crime occurred outside the building. This crime was also perpetrated upon large country houses and other buildings like museums or town halls, but in all cases, it was recorded as larceny and/or malicious damage even if a church was the victim.

So far as sacrilege was concerned, there were times when it was not recorded in the crime statistics as sacrilege. That happened because sacrilege was a very serious crime, equating with robbery, rape and murder, and it was more sensible to record some instances as simple larceny. This is the reason.

In 1968, the crime of sacrilege, along with many others, was removed from our statute book, but in my time at Aidensfield, it continued to feature in our criminal statistics as defined by Section 24 of the Larceny Act, 1916.

It was committed by any person who *broke and entered* a place of divine worship and committed any felony therein. It was also committed by those who broke out of any place of divine worship, having committed a felony therein.

A simple example would occur when a person opened the door of a church to gain entry and then stole candlesticks from the altar. By merely opening the door, they had 'broken' into the building. If the church door was standing open, however, and the thief simply walked through it and stole candlesticks, then it was not sacrilege. That would be simple larceny, or theft as it is now known.

The essence of the crime of sacrilege was breaking into the building – and the important factor was that the mere opening of a closed door or window was regarded as 'breaking'.

A felony included any serious crime like theft, rape, robbery or murder – so if a man opened the door of a church and went inside, then raped a woman at prayer, he would commit both rape and sacrilege, the sacrilege arising from the fact he had broken in and committed a felony, i.e., a serious crime, not necessarily one of stealing. The statute also catered for people who entered a church lawfully – perhaps to examine the premises – and then concealed themselves in order to steal something, later opening the door to leave or breaking out to escape.

In our training sessions, we argued the meaning of 'place of divine worship' and concluded it could apply to a tin shack if people gathered there for a divine service and it certainly included the churches or chapels of faiths other than the established Church of England.

We also learned that places within the church building, such as the vestry or bell tower, were regarded as 'a place of divine worship' so long as they were not structures quite separate from the church itself, in the style of some belfries or towers.

In deciding whether or not a crime should be recorded as sacrilege, a curious instance arose on the moors and it caused Sergeant Blaketon to worry about the meaning of 'place of divine worship'. One of the monks of Maddleskirk Abbey, Father Maurice, decided that he would like to live as a hermit. He had decided that the modern monks of the abbey, with their centrally heated cells, ready supply of food, access to cars, telephone and televisions, were not really living in the manner expected of a monk. Maurice, a sincere young fellow from Liverpool, was given permission by the abbot to occupy a cave on the moors above Lairsbeck, there to live like a hermit.

It would be for a trial period of six months. The Lairsbeck Cave had existed for thousands of years, and in the twelfth century had been home to a hermit called

Joseph; it had often been used as a temporary dwelling house by itinerants and in the seventeenth century it was occupied for several years by a man called Giles St George, who was not a monk. He had carved himself a table, chair and bed out of the solid limestone at the back of the cave, thus considerably extending the interior. The cave now had a lounge, bedroom and spare room at the back. When Giles left, no one else felt inclined to live in it and it survived as a curiosity.

With no doorway and open to all, these stone furnishings became a tourist attraction, and so the cave became well known to hikers, visitors, pilgrims and, sadly, vagrants, tramps, squatters and other unwelcome residents. Youngsters assembled there at weekends and used it for orgies and drinking parties before Lairsbeck Estate, which owned it, decided to instal a thick, heavy door. They fitted a solid wooden one which contained a small window. Visitors could peer inside at the renowned stone furniture, but were forbidden entry without express permission.

Thus the cave became secure from trespassers and wild animals. With the door in place, it was fairly cosy, being dry inside, cool in summer and warm in winter. It was to this place that Brother Maurice sallied forth full of prayer, worthy ideals and holy thoughts. He took few belongings, enough to dress and feed himself as well as the vessels and books necessary to say daily mass, and he did have the support of people who knew him. They would take him extra food if he needed it and in return, he would say mass for their intentions.

Skilled in self-sufficiency, he managed to survive on fruit, berries and wild creatures like rabbits and fish, his only modern concession being a small portable typewriter. He was to use this to keep notes about his experience, both from the practical and spiritual points of view. Then one day, when he was in the woods picking berries and inspecting his rabbit snares, someone sneaked into the cave and stole his typewriter. It was a couple of days before I was told – he had been out of the cave for about three hours, between 8.30 a.m. and 11.30 a.m., and had left the door closed, but unlocked.

He'd returned to find his precious typewriter missing – nothing else had been stolen.

'Shall I record it as sacrilege, Sergeant?' I put to Sergeant Blaketon when I returned to Ashfordly police station.

'Sacrilege? Don't be stupid, Rhea! That cave is not a place of divine worship!'

'It is,' I said. 'He's a fully ordained monk; he says mass there every day in a portion set aside as his personal chapel. His supporters are always welcome to join him at mass, as they sometimes do, so it is a church.'

'It's a dwelling house, Rhea. He lives there.'

'It's a cave, Sergeant.'

'Cave-breaking is not an offence under the Larceny Act, Rhea. People had stopped living in caves by the time it was enacted.'

'The crime at the cave was a breaking offence, Sergeant,' I said. 'Somebody opened the door, made an illegal entry and got away with his typewriter, worth twenty-five pounds.'

'I know it's a crime, Rhea, but what crime, precisely?'

'The typewriter was kept in the part he uses for mass, so it was sacrilege.' I didn't really believe what I was saying, but from time to time, did like to wind up Sergeant Blaketon, particularly so far as the interpretation of rules and regulations were concerned. 'It's more than mere simply larceny.'

'It's not burglary because it happened in the daylight hours,' he mused. 'I'd go for housebreaking, Rhea. It is a permanent structure and it is used as a dwelling house; tents, caravans and fairground booths are not permanent structures, Rhea, so they cannot be classified as dwelling houses, but this place is. Crime it as housebreaking.'

'Not storebreaking?' I said, tongue in cheek.

'Storebreaking?' boomed Blaketon.

'He keeps his belongings there....'

'You're playing games with me, Rhea!' he grinned. 'Housebreaking it is, not sacrilege, not burglary, not storebreaking, not warehousebreaking or not school-housebreaking.'

'How about officebreaking?' I smiled. 'Or pavilionbreaking, or workshopbreaking....'

'Housebreaking, Rhea!'

'Yes, Sergeant.'

We never traced Father Maurice's typewriter but the theft did highlight some of the legal fiction which was employed by the law, and further queries were raised about the precise meaning of 'place of divine worship'.

For example, there were some tricky questions about private chapels inside the great houses of this country and I cannot remember whether, if someone broke into such a chapel, it would constitute the offence of sacrilege or not. The question was whether a private chapel, deep within a large mansion, used wholly or mainly by the resident family and with access only through the mansion, was a place of divine worship. It was feasible that a visitor to the mansion could divert into the chapel for an unlawful purpose, and then steal something valuable from the altar. But would that be sacrilege? There was no offence of private chapelbreaking so what else could it be?

In the Middle Ages, the offence of sacrilege served as a protection of holy objects which were kept in a holy place. People who stole things like vestments, ornaments, chalices or any property belonging to the church were regarded as stealing from God, hence the seriousness of this crime. If someone stole an object left in the church by a worshipper, say a glove or a purse, the ancient law said this was not sacrilege but merely theft. Some tried to say the crime involved robbing a church, but the term 'robbery' suggests some kind of physical violence towards a person, and this was not present in most cases of theft from churches, such as galloping off with the candlesticks.

Other authorities felt the crime should be named burglary because it was breaking into the House of God, but sacrilege could be committed during the daylight hours, whilst (until 1968) burglary was limited to the night hours between 9 p.m. and 6 a.m.

Following a few centuries of debate, the crime of sacrilege was firmly placed on the English statute book in 1916 by the Larceny Act of that year and, upon reading the wording of the section, it extended the crime to protect *any* object within a place of divine worship. It was not restricted to holy or religious items used in church services. It could include the church bell, a grasscutter kept in the bell tower, hymn books, money placed in offertory boxes or even personal belongings left behind by a member of the congregation.

Quite simply, under the 1916 legislation, if someone broke into a place of divine worship and stole something, they committed the crime of sacrilege irrespective of the nature or value of the item taken.

The effect of this was that, on many occasions, country constables found themselves having to consider the crime of sacrilege whenever a parish church was raided by a thief or thieves. Bearing in mind that the crime carried a maximum sentence of life imprisonment, it was a very serious matter, and if lots of serious crimes filled the columns of our quarterly returns of crime statistics, it appeared that we were not doing our duty.

If, however, the church door was open to admit the felonious person or persons, then, if they stole something, the crime was simple larceny – this was a much lesser crime and looked far better in the crime statistics. It was amazing how many church doors were left open to admit thieves and thus make our crime statistics less alarming!

During my time at Aidensfield, my beat embraced several neighbouring villages which provided me with seven Anglican parish churches, five Catholic churches and a Catholic abbey containing an additional huge church, thirty-six chapels, six Methodist chapels, a Quaker meeting house, a Russian Orthodox church in a caravan, several private chapels in stately homes and castles, and sundry other places of divine worship including the hermit's cave. It was to be expected that I might have to deal with sacrilege from time to time, but in fact the incidence of sacrilege was very low while simple larceny from churches was fairly common.

This was because the church doors were open to admit the wrongdoers, which, it could be argued, is the reason for the existence of the churches. The idea was that they should not sin while inside; however, unfortunately, many did. They were quite capable of stealing anything from cassocks to hassocks.

Beyond all doubt, the most common crime inside a church was larceny of cash from offertory boxes. Many offertory boxes were nothing more than wooden containers with a slot in the lid to admit the money, and these were placed near the entrance in the hope that casual visitors or regular worshippers would contribute some of their cash towards the upkeep of the building. Thieves would often steal the entire thing to break it open at their leisure; some offertory boxes were later fixed to the walls or the back of a bench and the thieves upgraded their efforts by prising them off with large screwdrivers or jemmies. Later, metal offertory boxes were built into the walls, and so the thieves used even more powerful tools to remove them and break them open for their contents.

One problem for the police was that no one knew precisely how much cash was in an offertory box when it was stolen, or whether the haul comprised notes or coins. Guesswork, or to be official, estimating the loss, was therefore part of the routine in such cases, the vicar and the police between them estimating the contents of a box by taking an average income over a number of days. The average cash theft was around £2, but we did find that if the offertory box at All Saints, Aidensfield was broken into, you could guarantee that St Aidan's was raided the same day, and that other nearby churches were also attacked.

Travelling offertory box raiders were usually responsible, their daily takings amounting to a considerable sum following their visits to a sequence of rural churches. Such raids would happen only once a year or so but I have never known the theft of the contents of an offertory box be classified as sacrilege. According to police records, the doors were always open to admit the thieves.

The other things that were regularly stolen were brass candlesticks from the altar but from time to time, more valuable items were removed, such as antique chairs, silver chalices and other treasures or collectables. Some churches kept a safe in the vestry, inside which there might be communion wine, the chalice, the silver plate used during the service and other church valuables. Thieves would smash their way into the church at night and remove the safe, or blow it open if they thought it contained a lot of treasures. In such cases, the crime was recorded as sacrilege.

Bearing in mind the complexities of recording the crime of sacrilege, one problem arose at Thackerston's ancient church. The vicar, The Reverend Norman Dunn, lived at Crampton Vicarage, and Thackerston was within his parish; both places were on my beat. Dunn was a fairly new arrival at Crampton, having come from Doncaster.

'Someone's taking the flowers from the altar,' he told me one morning.

'It'll be the flower ladies, surely?' I said. 'Removing those which are jaded.'

'That's what I thought. I've asked them: they're as baffled as me,' admitted The Reverend Dunn. 'We make sure the altar flowers for the Sunday service are fresh, and they remain on the altar until they need replacing. Some last longer than others, as you'll appreciate. But sometimes when I walk in to the church on a morning, perhaps on a Tuesday or a Wednesday, the vases have been emptied. It's been happening for a few weeks now, Mr Rhea, I've been keeping observations. Five bunches of narcissi disappeared after last Sunday. I noticed their absence on Tuesday. These are good flowers, not dead ones.'

'How can someone walk off with flowers and not be seen? When are they being taken?'

'Overnight, I'm sure. I close the church door at ten each evening, and open it at seven, give or take a few minutes. We never lock the door, by the way, the church is always open for visitors, night and day, even when the door is closed.'

I groaned inwardly. This was another case of sacrilege. To break into a church, i.e. by merely opening the door, and then steal anything inside, fulfilled the legal definition, even if it was just a few flowers.

'Rhea,' said Sergeant Blaketon when I told him, 'there is no way I am going to crime the theft of a few penn'orth of flowers as sacrilege! It's like taking the proverbial sledgehammer to crack a nut.'

'But that's what the law says, Sergeant. We don't make the law, we merely uphold it. The fact is that someone is going into that church at night and stealing flowers which have been paid for out of church funds. Legally, that is sacrilege.'

'There are times the law is an ass. You'd better make more enquiries, Rhea, before we bring the full majesty of English law on to this nighttime narcissus nicker. Anyway, how can we prove the door was not standing open to admit the thief?'

I had no intention of sitting in Thackerston Church all night with a view to arresting the flower thief, even if his activities did constitute one of the more serious crimes against English law, so I began to make discreet enquiries in Thackerston. I concentrated upon members of the congregation, trying to learn something about their activities and personalities, and it wasn't long before I discovered a story concerning an elderly lady called Elsie Parry. A stalwart of the church, flower lady, hymn-book dispenser and bell-ringer on occasions, she had been taken ill with a heart complaint and was in Eltering Hospital.

She and her husband, Stanley, lived in a tiny cottage at Thackerston, a cottage with no garden, I learned, and it didn't take me long to learn that her bedside at the hospital was always rich with flowers. I went to see Stanley whom I had encountered many times during my visits to the village – prior to his retirement, he used to be the lengthman, keeping the roads clean, tidy and in state of good repair. We often had a chat over a cup of tea at his neat cottage and he was not surprised when I popped in for a word with him.

'Stanley,' I said. 'How's Elsie?'

'Coping well, Mr Rhea, but not likely to come home. She's very frail, but she's had a good life.'

'You get to see her, do you?'

'Aye,' he said. 'On t'bus. I get in most days.'

'I heard she likes flowers,' I said gently.

'Loves 'em,' he spoke quietly. 'But without a garden, I can't grow any. I take her them from t'church, after Sundays. They"re no use to anybody then, nobody goes in to see 'em. It's a waste, eh?'

'What's a waste, Stanley?'

'Spending good money on flowers for t'altar and then letting 'em die with nobody else seeing 'em. Tourists never notice 'em. Elsie allus loved her flowers; she brought 'em home after t'services, t'old vicar said she could ... she loves flowers, you see, Mr Rhea, allus has done.'

'Give her my regards.' I departed after we'd had a cup of tea together and went to see The Reverend Dunn. I told him about Stanley and discovered that the outgoing vicar had never thought to mention the destination of the Sunday flowers, but when I explained things, Dunn grimaced.

'You know, Mr Rhea, I have been to the hospital to visit Elsie and did admire the flowers ... she never said where they had come from! But I will ensure she is never without any, and I will visit Stanley too.'

'Don't tell him I almost arrested him for committing sacrilege, will you?' I pleaded.

'Of course not,' he laughed. 'But how can we correct things with the law?'

'Correct things?' I puzzled.

'Didn't I report a case of sacrilege to you?'

'All I need from you is an assurance that you have given Stanley permission to remove the flowers, and I'll ensure he is not sentenced to life imprisonment.'

'Done,' he said.

I explained to Sergeant Blaketon that the outgoing vicar had not acquainted his successor with all the minutiae of parish life, and that there had been no case of sacrilege at Thackerston.

' "We have legalized confiscation, consecrated sacrilege and condoned high treason",' smiled Sergeant Blaketon.

'Pardon?' I wondered if I had heard him correctly.

'Benjamin Disraeli,' he said. 'In one of his speeches to the House of Commons.'

'Fancy that,' I said, taking my leave.

Another interesting case of sacrilege occurred in a tiny, but fascinating church on my patch at Briggsby. It occupies a hilltop site but in former times, stood in a field about two miles away, it was then the private chapel of the ancient Briggsby Hall. In 1797, Briggsby Hall was destroyed by fire and in later years, some of its outbuildings were used by a local farmer to house his cattle, pigs and poultry, as well as the storage of agricultural machinery. Having become redundant as a chapel, this particular building was used as a barn, but in the nineteenth century it was demolished and the stones were used to build the present church.

Some of the internal woodwork dates from its days as a chapel, but this lovely somewhat modern church is very small. With only twelve benches, one dedicated to each apostle, it can only accommodate sixty people, i.e five to a bench.

Its main attraction is a remarkable collection of hassocks. In the North Riding of Yorkshire, hassock was the word for a footstool without any feet or legs, and these cushion-like objects were variously known as hussocks or hossacks depending upon which part of the county one happened to be. More widely, hassock is the name applied to small cushions upon which to kneel in church, these are often known simply as kneelers, but the Briggsby collection of hassocks was renowned. There was a total of sixty, one for each seat in the church, and they were unusual because they had been made by sixty ladies of the parish in 1918 to mark the end of the First World War. Each was exactly the same size – fifteen inches long by eight inches broad and four inches deep, and every one had been embroidered with a different design and colours, albeit with every one of them incorporating the word 'Peace' and the date '1918'.

Some bore depictions of saints or flowers or animals, others had the names of local soldiers lost in that awful war, one had an embroidered picture of Briggsby church, another showed the Crucifixion and yet another the Last Supper, but each was quite distinct in its character and each adornment had been chosen by the lady who had made it. In some cases, they had included their initials, discreetly hidden among the embroidery work. As a collection, therefore, they were probably unique – certainly, I had never come across such a beautiful set of kneelers.

And then one of them disappeared. It was the church warden, Jeremy Newton, who told me. I was patrolling Briggsby on foot one fresh Saturday morning in April and saw him emerging from the little church.

'Morning, Mr Newton,' I called. He was retired and looked like a former brigadier, a tall slim gentleman who was invariably smartly dressed in rustic tweeds and who sported a clipped moustache and a trim hairstyle.

'Ah, good morning, Constable,' he smiled as he came towards me. 'Just the fellow!'

'Something wrong?' I could see the look of concern on his face.

'I'm not sure.' He rubbed his chin, then said, 'Come inside, I'll show you something.'

He led me into the small, rather dark interior of the little church and indicated the hassocks which were positioned upon each seat, ready for use. He asked if I knew their history. I said I did.

'There's one missing,' he said, pointing to one of the pews. 'There should be five on each pew, but this pew – dedicated to the apostle Peter – has only four.'

I glanced at the others and did a quick count; he was right. There were fifty-nine hassocks instead of the required sixty.

'You've searched the church?' I put to him. 'Vestry. Store-room? Tower? Under the pews? All likely hiding places?'

'Everywhere, several times,' he said. 'They are quite large, as you can see, so they're not easily overlooked. And, I might add, no one has any authority to remove any of the hassocks without the consent of the vicar.'

'And he has not given any such permission?'

'No, I rang him this morning, to tell him, and he has not given his permission to anyone but he can't say when they were last counted or checked.'

'So when did it vanish?' was my next question.

'That's the problem. It's hard to say, Mr Rhea. We rarely, if ever, count them, you see. On a day-to-day basis, we'd never notice that just one was missing. It was only that we had all the pews revarnished on Monday and Tuesday which meant removing all the hassocks beforehand, then I volunteered to replace them this morning. I was counting them out, five per pew, when I discovered the deficiency.'

'Was it there when the hassocks were removed prior to the revarnishing?' I asked him.

'I didn't undertake that chore,' he said. 'Mrs Grieves – she's the organist – picked them all up and stored them in the vestry after the services last Sunday.'

'You mentioned it to her?'

'Yes, I did. As well as the vicar. Sadly, she can't say whether one was missing then or not when she collected them.'

'So it could have been taken at any time, even during the last year or even longer ago?'

'I'm afraid so, Mr Rhea.'

'And that makes tracing it a very difficult task, Mr Newton. But it seems odd that only one has gone – if a determined or knowledgeable thief was responsible, you'd think he would have taken the lot, the entire collection.'

'Those were my thoughts,' he acknowledged. 'Except that you'd need a van or large car to carry them all away at one go. You can pop one of them in a carrier bag, that way you could remove them all day by day, over a period of time.'

'So what's it look like, the missing hassock?' I continued.

He blushed. 'I don't know,' he admitted. 'We've never kept a record of them; I have no idea which one is missing. All I can say is that it is the same size as the others which are left, with colourful embroidered markings upon it along with the date 1918 and the word "Peace".'

'So,' I said, 'we have a missing hassock, description unknown, which disappeared on an unknown date? No one knows when it was last seen....'

'True,' he said, rather sheepishly.

'If I am to treat this as a crime, I need to be certain that it has been stolen, Mr Newton. It could be lost or mislaid, for example. The passage of time and lack of certainty about its last known presence would suggest that. You see, if we do decide it has been stolen by a thief who opened the door to get into your church, then the crime would be sacrilege – which carries a maximum sentence of life imprisonment!'

'Good grief!' his eyes opened wide. 'That serious, is it?'

'Stealing from churches is serious,' I said. 'And good old English law continues to regard sacrilege as a most serious offence. Perhaps a further search of the church? Have you asked any of the other parishioners? After all, there is a very small congregation.'

'That is a somewhat delicate matter, Mr Rhea. As you know, the hassocks were made by the ladies of this parish, as a kind of war memorial, and many of their descendants continue to live here and to worship at this church. If they thought that someone was stealing the hassocks, they'd come and remove all those which remain – then we'd have none.'

'You'd have none if a thief came and stole the lot!' I remarked.

'I did wonder if the thief would return – you know, to take one at a time.'

'I am still not sure that the missing one has been stolen,' I said. 'I think that if a thief was at work, you'd have lost more than a single hassock. After all, we have no idea when it was taken, so, clearly, no one has missed it until today. Now, have you mentioned it to anyone else?'

'Apart from the vicar and Mrs Grieves, no.'

'Right,' I said. 'I don't think Sergeant Blaketon would allow me to treat this as the crime of sacrilege. Although it is missing, there's no proof it has been stolen and we have

no idea when it was taken, or when it was last in its place.
It's all too vague, Mr Newton.'

'So you can't help?' There was almost a plea in his voice.

'Not officially,' I offered. 'But if you like, I can ask
discreet questions around the village, to see if anyone
might have removed it for any reason?'

'Well, I'm not sure if you should do that. I don't want to
start a panic in Briggsby and have worried relatives
coming to remove the lot.'

'Who comes to work in the church, apart from yourself
and Mrs Grieves?' I asked.

'Mrs Bingley, she's the cleaner, and Miss Dale, she sees
to the flowers.'

'Right, what I propose to do is to pop into the church for
a quiet word with one or other of those two ladies. I'll do it
when I'm passing, ostensibly a casual visit, and I'll
pretend I am interested in the hassocks. That way, I can
quiz them to see if they know anything. And I'll keep you
informed – but I don't think I should crime this one just
yet, Mr Newton. I should hate one of your parishioners to
be made liable to life imprisonment!'

'As you say, Mr Rhea.'

'And can you do one thing to help us in the future?'

'Yes, of course!'

'Make an inventory of all the items in the church,
especially those hassocks, with a detailed description of
each one. You might even consider drawings or
photographs, just in case any more go missing.'

'Yes, yes, of course. An excellent idea, Mr Rhea.'

My offer to help was probably highly unofficial but I
knew that Sergeant Blaketon and the CID would never
accept the disappearance of the Briggsby hassock as a
genuine crime, nor could we circulate a description in an
attempt to trace it. We had no idea what it looked like,
other than an indication of its size and shape. And to have
the crime categorized as sacrilege would cause the CID
admin. office at Headquarters to regard us as a joke.

Nonetheless, I did feel some responsibility towards the
parishioners of Briggsby, hence my action. My opportunity to help came about three weeks later when I noticed

Mrs Bingley sweeping the steps which led into the church. The door was wide open as I parked my minivan and went across. She was a plump, jolly lady in her late sixties and wore an overall pinny as she went about her voluntary chores.

'Morning, Mrs Bingley,' I greeted her.

'Now then, Mr Rhea. I thought I'd do a bit of spring cleaning. You'd never believe how mucky a church can get.'

'I saw the door was open so I thought I'd have a look at the famous hassocks,' I began.

'Help yourself.' She waved towards the door and continued with her sweeping. Inside, I looked once more upon the hassocks – and the rear pew had four, not five. All the others bore five hassocks – eleven with five, and one with four, a total of fifty-nine. One of them was still missing.

'Nice, aren't they?' She had come into the church with her broom in her hands. 'You know the history?'

'Yes, I've heard a lot about them and thought it would be nice to have a look at them. There's one missing, though,' and I pointed to the empty space. 'Shouldn't there be sixty?'

'It's been missing for ages,' she said. 'For as long as I've been doing cleaning. Three years and a bit, that'll be.'

'It's a shame,' I said. 'It makes the collection incomplete.'

'Well, it's always been like that so far as I know. I read somewhere there should be sixty, but I can't remember when they were all here and I've lived here all my life. There's always been one missing since I started the cleaning job, and probably long before that.'

'So nobody's shown any concern?'

'No, nobody ever counts 'em, Mr Rhea.'

After passing the time of day with her and looking at some of the other objects of interest, I left the church, happy that I had not treated the missing hassock with the seriousness of the crime of sacrilege. Quite literally, it could be anywhere whether or not anyone had stolen it.

Five or six weeks passed before I noticed Jeremy

Newton's car outside the church and so I halted for an update. I had gleaned nothing useful, but there were limits as to my investigative brief. I went in and found him counting hymn books. It seemed there was to be a wedding the coming Saturday.

'Ah, Mr Rhea,' he smiled. 'Hassock-hunting, I hear?'

I told him about my conversation with Mrs Bingley, but she had clearly had words with him about it, and he added, 'We're getting organized now, Mr Rhea. I have done an inventory of the church – everything from pews to pewter, in a manner of speaking, and I have included the hassocks, all fifty-nine of them.'

At that point, he delved into a brief case which lay on a table at the back of the church and produced a colourful chart which listed all the hassocks; someone had reproduced the designs in colour and so he now had an excellent source of reference.

'See,' he said, walking across to one of the pews. 'I can check them off one by one against this list, so if another goes, we'll know what it looks like.'

'I like that one,' I said, pointing to the drawing upon a pictured hassock. It portrayed the Virgin Mary cradling Christ in her arms after He had been taken down from the cross.

'It was over there,' he said, indicating the Matthew seat. 'But they do get moved around; they don't occupy a particular place, you understand. The cleaner moves them as do the congregation....'

I went into the pew to look at the artistry on the hassock I had admired, but failed to find it. I looked in all the other pews, but it was not there.

'It's not here, Mr Newton.' I felt a sense of dread.

'It must be!' he said. 'It was here when I finalized this inventory a couple of nights ago ... let me check for you....'

But there was no sign of it. I counted the hassocks. There were fifty-nine of them.

For a few seconds, I was baffled and then I said, 'Which of these here present was not here when you compiled your inventory, can you tell?'

'It'll take a while,' he said, but he began by calling out a description from his list. As he called out the descriptions, I turned each of the hassocks upside down to show they had been accounted for. Finally, we were left with one which was not on his list. It showed a Christmas scene, with the Child Jesus in the manger and the animals all around. I picked it up and looked at it.

'It's been repaired,' I said. 'You can see the new embroidery work … see, here?'

He screwed up his eyes and said, 'By jove, yes! So this one has been taken away by somebody, repaired and replaced!'

'Yes,' I said. 'And when returning this one, they have taken another for repair, the one I was looking for. I've no idea how long such a task would take, but I would imagine quite a long time.'

I lifted several of the others and, upon close examination, it was possible to see that recent repairs had been made to some of them. It was evident that someone was secretly repairing all the hassocks, one by one, and thus for a long time, there'd be fifty-nine in church and one elsewhere. So long as the phantom repairer was at work, there would be fifty-nine hassocks in church.

'You'd better add the nativity scene to your list,' I said to Mr Newton.

'It would be sacrilege to omit it!' he smiled.

I never did find out who was making those skilled repairs but, on reflection, it wasn't my duty to do so. But if you pop into that church today, all sixty hassocks are in position, each neatly repaired.